"We're Not Going To Fall In Love,"

Jake said in a voice as warm and soft as melted butter. "I won't break your heart—you won't break mine."

"You sound so sure of yourself," Maggie said, annoyed by his confidence. She was aware of his hands on her waist, his closeness, the faint scent of his aftershave. Jake was a wanderer. If she didn't want to risk falling in love with him, she should stay clear away from him. But his confidence made her feel suddenly reckless, and she slanted him a look, sliding her hand to the back of his neck.

"You're so certain you won't fall in love with me," she said softly. "Maybe you should guard *your* heart." She stood on tiptoe and placed her lips boldly on his. She saw the startled flicker in his dark eyes before she closed her eyes and poured her heart into the kiss.

Dear Reader,

What could be more satisfying than the sinful yet guilt-free pleasure of enjoying six new passionate, powerful and provocative Silhouette Desire romances this month?

Get started with *In Blackhawk's Bed*, July's MAN OF THE MONTH and the latest title in the SECRETS! miniseries by Barbara McCauley. *The Royal & the Runaway Bride* by Kathryn Jensen—in which the heroine masquerades as a horse trainer and becomes a princess—is the seventh exciting installment in DYNASTIES: THE CONNELLYS, about an American family that discovers its royal roots.

A single mom melts the steely defenses of a brooding ranch hand in *Cowboy's Special Woman* by Sara Orwig, while a detective with a secret falls for an innocent beauty in *The Secret Millionaire* by Ryanne Corey. A CEO persuades a mail-room employee to be his temporary wife in the debut novel *Cinderella & the Playboy* by Laura Wright, praised by *New York Times* bestselling author Debbie Macomber as "a wonderful new voice in Silhouette Desire." And in *Zane: The Wild One* by Bronwyn Jameson, the mayor's daughter turns up the heat on the small town's bad boy made good.

So pamper the romantic in you by reading all six of these great new love stories from Silhouette Desire!

Enjoy!

Joan Marlow Golan

Joan Marlow Golan
Senior Editor, Silhouette Desire

Please address questions and book requests to:
Silhouette Reader Service
U.S.: 3010 Walden Ave., P.O. Box 1325, Buffalo, NY 14269
Canadian: P.O. Box 609, Fort Erie, Ont. L2A 5X3

Cowboy's Special Woman

Woman

SARA ORWIG

Silhouette® Desire,

Published by Silhouette Books
America's Publisher of Contemporary Romance

SILHOUETTE BOOKS

ISBN 0-373-76449-9

COWBOY'S SPECIAL WOMAN

Visit Silhouette at www.eHarlequin.com

Printed in U.S.A.

Books by Sara Orwig

Silhouette Desire

Falcon's Lair #938
The Bride's Choice #1019
A Baby for Mommy #1060
Babes in Arms #1094
Her Torrid Temporary Marriage #1125
The Consummate Cowboy #1164
The Cowboy's Seductive Proposal #1192
World's Most Eligible Texan #1346
Cowboy's Secret Child #1368
The Playboy Meets His Match #1438
Cowboy's Special Woman #1449

Silhouette Intimate Moments

Hide in Plain Sight #679
Galahad in Blue Jeans #971

SARA ORWIG

lives with her husband and children in Oklahoma. She has a patient husband who will take her on research trips anywhere, from big cities to old forts. She is an avid collector of Western history books. With a master's degree in English, Sara writes historical romance, mainstream fiction and contemporary romance. Books are beloved treasures that take Sara to magical worlds, and she loves both reading and writing them.

With thanks to my editors
Joan Marlow Golan and Julie Barrett

One

There weren't many things that could tie him in knots, but fire was one. Jake Reiner held his Harley with a white-knuckled grip and glanced over his shoulder at flames whipping through cedars and oaks. In spite of the hundred-degree August heat and blasts of hot Oklahoma wind, he was chilled by the sight of the fire. He knew he was racing along the dusty road at a dangerous speed, but he had to warn the ranch family who lived at the end of the lane.

In minutes he came roaring up from a dip in the road, took a curve and saw a tall two-story Victorian house ahead. Shade trees surrounded a three-car garage, a brown barn, a bunkhouse, sheds and a corral. A Circle A brand was burned in the wood above the barn door. Inside the fenced yard, a woman stepped around the thick trunk of a giant cottonwood tree. In her hand she held a power saw.

Jake's gaze raked over a figure that made his pulse skip. Cutoffs hugged trim hips and revealed long, shapely legs. Stretching snugly over lush breasts, a T-shirt was tucked into the waistband of the cutoffs. His gaze swept up to her face as he approached. She looked wary. Long, golden hair was in a thick braid that hung down her back to her waist.

Barking a warning, a black-and-tan dog ran around the barn. The woman's head snapped around and she spoke to the dog. Stopping beside her, it continued barking.

Jake slowed and braked, sending up a flurry of dust. As the engine idled, he braced his legs. Then he heard a child's cries. Following the sound, he looked at the cottonwood. Perched on a lower limb was a small girl with a gash on her head and tears streaking her cheeks.

"Mommy!"

"Hold on, Katy," the woman said calmly. Glaring at Jake, she snapped, "What do you want?"

"Can I help?" he asked, getting off the bike, realizing that, between the fire and whatever was happening here, this family had real trouble. At the moment, the child seemed the most urgent problem.

"Why are you here?" the woman asked, her cautious demeanor transforming to anger. As he watched sparks dancing in her blue eyes, he knew he didn't give a reassuring appearance with his shaggy hair, his bike, and his ragged jeans.

"Up by the road your place is on fire."

While her gaze flew past him, the color drained from her face.

"Not now!" she gasped and looked up at the

child. "I have to get Katy free first." She turned away as if she had already forgotten his presence.

Moving closer to the tree and forgetting the stranger, Maggie Langford fought a rising panic. Katy was caught and hurting, and now their place was on fire. A really bad fire would devastate them. She said a small prayer that she could free Katy's foot, which was wedged between a limb and the trunk. As Maggie raised the heavy saw, a hand closed around her wrist and the stranger took the saw from her.

For a split second, with the physical contact, an electric current of awareness zipped through her. When the stranger stepped closer, Katy let out a howl.

"I'll just cut a little more, and then I can break that limb free. You get up there and hold her so she doesn't fall," he said in a deep voice.

"Hang on, Katy, I'm coming up beside you," Maggie said, trying to calm her child.

"This is my little tomboy," she told the stranger. "Katy was climbing and fell. Shh, Katy. It'll be all right. You'll be loose soon," Maggie said.

"Have to watch these trees. They'll just reach out and grab you," the stranger said to Katy with a reassuring smile that softened his rugged features.

Through tears and the streaks of blood from the head wound, Katy smiled in return.

Maggie caught a limb and pulled herself up, taking hold of her five-year-old. Katy twisted to cling to her.

Maggie looked down at the tall, deeply tanned man. His shaggy black hair hung below the red bandanna wound around his head. He wore a black T-shirt with the sleeves ripped away, and thick mus-

cles flexed as he sawed the limb. The loud buzz of
the saw was the only sound until he stopped, set
down the saw and glanced up at her with his dark
eyes.

"Ready?"

She nodded. "Hang on to me, Katy," she said,
holding her daughter.

The stranger jumped up, grasped the limb and
hung on it. With a sharp crack the limb split from
the tree, freeing Katy's foot. As agile as a cat, the
stranger landed on his feet and tossed the limb aside.

Katy's arms tightened around Maggie's neck, and
Maggie held her tightly in return, relieved to have
her daughter safe again. Then the stranger reached
up. "Hand her to me."

Maggie passed her daughter down. The stranger
set her gently on the ground and Katy rubbed her
ankle and sniffed. Maggie swung her legs over the
limb to jump down. As she jumped, hands came
around her waist and the stranger caught her. Without thought she put her hands out to grip his arms,
feeling the rock-solid muscles, looking into brown
eyes that bored into her with an electrifying intensity.
The instant her hands had closed on his arms, a current had raced through her. Unable to breathe or look
away, she stared back at him while her heart ham-
mered. He smelled faintly of sweat and aftershave.
The aftershave surprised her. He looked primitive
rather than civilized, yet she knew she was rushing
to judge too swiftly.

He lowered her to the ground and for seconds she
was still caught and held in his compelling gaze.

"Mommy."

Her daughter's voice released her from the spell,

and Maggie stepped back, dropping her hands to her sides. "Thanks again, mister. I have to call 911 and alert them about the fire."

She knelt beside her daughter. "Let me see your ankle, Katy." She was aware that the stranger watched while she checked Katy's bruised and scratched ankle. She moved her daughter's foot gently. "That hurt?"

"No."

"Katy, you should thank the man," Maggie said as she stood.

"Thank you, sir," Katy said politely, sniffing and rubbing her ankle as she tried to stand. Maggie swung her up into her arms.

"My name is Jake Reiner," the stranger said in a voice that stirred a curl of warmth in Maggie. Once more she was riveted by his gaze. With an effort she broke away, turning toward the house. She waved her hand toward the barn. "There's a spigot. You might like a cold drink. I've got a fire to fight. Thanks for alerting me about it. C'mon, Tuffy," she commanded, and the dog trotted at her heels.

She shifted the child and headed for the house as Jake watched, fascinated. Her hips swayed slightly and her cutoffs were short enough to give him a delectable view of long legs. He stood staring at her until the screen door slapped shut behind her.

When he glanced back up the lane to the southwest, Jake saw a plume of gray smoke rising over the treetops, the high wind swirling it away. This ranch family was in deep trouble.

Between the garage and the barn, Jake spotted the faucet and strolled toward it. When he passed the garage and glanced inside, he saw a pickup and a

battered flatbed truck that had once been black but
had lost most of its paint. Turning the spigot, he
splashed cold water over his head. As he ran his fingers through his hair, he looked into the barn that
stood open to his left. The barn was filled with a
clutter of tack and large trunks. He glanced from the
barn to his bike, which held most of his worldly pos-
sessions. At least with his wandering lifestyle, he
didn't have to mend, repair or care for a lot of things.
He bent to take another long drink and splash more
water on himself. As he straightened, a pickup bar-
reled up the road and rocked to a stop, sending up a
thick plume of red dust. A brown-haired woman
jumped out and glanced at Jake.

"Is Maggie inside?" she asked as she ran around
the pickup.

When he nodded, she moved faster, sprinting to
the house and reaching for the screen door without
knocking. In seconds the blonde appeared, unhooked
the screen, which Jake assumed had been secured
because of his presence. The brunette stepped inside
while the blonde came out. He saw the brunette hook
the screen and look at him a moment, but then his
gaze shifted to the blonde. She hurried toward him,
her breasts bouncing with each step.

"Have to get to the fire," she said as she passed
him and headed into the garage.

In its dim interior she grabbed a shovel and tossed
it into the bed of a pickup where it landed with a
clang.

Jake moved into the garage, feeling the coolness
when he stepped out of the sunlight. "Can I help?"

"Grab those gunnysacks, wet them down and
throw them in the pickup," she ordered while she

ran toward the barn. He spotted empty gunnysacks hanging on a hook. Lifting them down, he carried them to the faucet. As soon as they were soaked, he tossed them into the back of the pickup. She threw more shovels into the back.

"Thanks, again, mister."

"Sure," he said, opening the pickup door for her. "And you can call me Jake," he added.

She gave him a quick nod. With another flash of her long legs, she climbed inside. In spite of the fire, the rancher who lived here was a lucky man with a pretty wife and a cute little daughter. Jake was surprised at his sentiments. He valued his freedom enough that he didn't usually view anyone who was married and settled as lucky. He closed the pickup door and turned to go to his bike.

As the pickup raced past him, he waited, letting the dust settle before he followed.

Overhead a gray cloud of smoke spread in the sky and his sympathy for her increased. The south wind was blowing the fire north toward her house. He rounded a bend and smoke rolled over the road, engulfing him. As he drove through it, he held his breath. When the world became a dense gray blur that stung his eyes and burned his throat, panic threatened. He knew the rule: don't drive into smoke. But he had driven into it and now he had to keep going. He could feel the heat of the fire and hear its roar. Then, as he reached the backside of the smoke and fire, he could see again.

Gulping fresh air, he was stunned by the magnitude of the fire that raged out of control, stretching across the land with acres of burning trees and grass. Cars lined the county road as men worked to beat out the flames. Someone had parked a flatbed truck near the firefighters and in the back of the truck were three large orange coolers and a stack of paper cups. Jake wondered how all these people had learned about the fire so quickly, but he assumed word spread fast and neighbors rushed to help out.

Two pumper trucks were driving along the perimeter of the fire, the firemen pouring gushing silver streams of water on the line of flames, but the strong wind was fanning the fire furiously and their effort seemed futile. Accentuated by pops and crackles, the blaze roared while heat waves shimmered in the hot summer air.

Jake spotted the blonde, already in the line of men fighting the fire with shovels and gunnysacks. She was working as hard as any man around her, swinging a gunnysack and beating flames. While dread and sorrow tore at him, Jake parked in the line of pickups.

Jogging back up the road, he spotted a shovel in the bed of a pickup. Grabbing the shovel, Jake fell into line with the volunteers, moving to the edge of the fire to try to smother the bright orange flames while heat buffeted him.

As he inhaled the stinging smoke, his mind jumped back in time. Hating the tormenting memories of that long-ago fire, he dug with fury.

In the flickering orange, he saw himself as a boy, running and looking at a glow in the sky. Deep in the black hours of early morning, coming home across backyards, he had seen pink light the night sky. As he drew nearer to it, the first fear gripped him and then he was racing, bursting around the corner and tearing across the street toward his home that was a roaring blaze lighting up the entire block.

While the raging inferno consumed his house, he tried to run inside and firemen held him back. Over his yelling, he finally heard their shouts. How long did it take him to realize they were telling him his family was dead? Still, all these years later, a knot tightened in Jake's throat. He hated his vulnerability, and thought he had succeeded in keeping his feelings tightly locked away, yet this burning wall of flame brought the horror and hurt back. With the fire dancing in front of him, its flames taunting him, the years vanished and the pain he had felt that night consumed him. Tears streaked his cheeks. Harder and faster he dug as if physical labor could erase the aching memories and the screaming guilt.

A man passed him. "Ease up, son. If you don't slow, we'll be carrying you away. I'm taking water to everyone."

Facing Jake was a tall, brown-haired man in ragged overalls. He held a water cooler and a tin cup.

"You're Jake Reiner, aren't you?"

"Yes, sir. Thanks." Jake filled the cup and drank, not caring that it was a communal cup.

"I'm Ben Alden. I've seen you ride."

"Thanks for the water," Jake said, returning the cup. The man nodded and moved down the line. Jake glanced along the row and saw the blonde talking to the man. She turned back to fight the fire.

Soon it seemed as if he had been fighting fire for hours. As sweat poured off his body, smoke burned his eyes and throat. Around him men yelled, and he could hear the rumble of the pumper trucks over the crackle and roar of the fire.

With his muscles screaming, Jake looked around and saw the blonde talking to Ben Alden again, the man who had carried the water around earlier. The man had his big, work-reddened hands on her shoulders.

Watching the man touch her possessively, Jake had an uncustomary annoyance and couldn't understand his reaction. He didn't even know the woman's name and would never see her again after this morning, but he wished he could push Ben Alden's hands off of her shoulders. Alden was probably her husband. Jake stared at the tall, rawboned man who was much older than she was. His brown hair was streaked with gray. He was solid muscle on big bones. He wore a T-shirt beneath coveralls. Then Jake noticed their profiles, the same straight noses and broad foreheads and he wondered if the man was her father.

Taking a deep breath, Jake returned to digging, throwing dirt on the fire, watching the flames spread with each gust of wind. Now three pumper trucks were working along the backside of the fire, but in spite of everyone's efforts, they weren't bringing the blaze under control. Long ago Jake had shed his shirt and sweat poured off his body. He thought of ice and longed for a cold shower and a cold drink.

The ranch house and other buildings were in view now. Choking and coughing, he felt on fire. His hands were raw, and he had to stop for water. He headed toward the flatbed truck with the water coolers, reaching first to pour a bucket of water over himself.

He spotted the blonde, still struggling to swing a gunnysack and he suspected she must be about to drop from the exertion. He picked up a paper cup and the cooler and walked over to her, catching her arm.

She turned, her face smudged with soot. Her T-shirt was plastered to her body from perspiration. Wordlessly he filled the cup and held it out to her. She looked dazed, and he took her arm to lead her to the pickup.

With shaking hands, she grasped the cup and gulped the water. ''Thanks,'' she said, staring at him while he tilted the cooler and refilled her cup.

''Maybe you should go up to your house and get your little girl out of there and save what you can.''

''Shortly after I left, my sister Patsy took Katy and Tuffy, our dog, to her house. She packed some of Katy's things.'' Maggie looked at the fire. ''I'm needed more here.''

''We're not going to stop it,'' Jake said. ''Go save some of your clothes and furniture. I'll drive you up there and help. Come on. None of us can stop this inferno unless it rains or the wind changes and those possibilities look unlikely.''

When he took her arm, she hesitated. ''Come on,'' he urged. In silence she walked with him. ''Which pickup is yours?'' he asked.

She stared at him blankly and then looked around, pointing to a black pickup parked in a line of pickups. ''Keys,'' he said, holding out his hand.

''I can drive.''

''Give me the keys. You can catch your breath.''

As she handed over the keys, they walked to the pickup. He drove through a wall of smoke again until they were beyond it.

"Our house," she said softly as they approached her home. "My grandfather built this house."

"Was that your husband you were talking to?"

"No." Her head swung around and she looked at him for a moment as if she had to think back to remember. "He's my father. My husband and I are divorced."

"Sorry."

"I came back home last year to live with my dad when my mother died."

"I don't know your name."

"Maggie Langford."

"I met your dad when he brought me some water. He's Ben Alden," he said and she nodded. Jake pulled to a stop by the back door and climbed out. She was already out and sprinting for the back door.

"Anything in particular I can get for you?"

"Yes. If we can save it, there's some furniture that has been handed down through the generations."

When he followed her inside, all her dazed manner vanished as she began to briskly issue orders.

As he secured the last bit of a second load of scrapbooks, clothing and furniture, Jake glanced over his shoulder and his stomach knotted at the proximity of the blaze. The house, barn and all outbuildings seemed doomed. He heard an engine and when he looked around, the three pumper trucks came down the lane, and her father drove a tractor along the side of the road. Firemen spilled from the trucks and ran to the house with fire retardant blankets to toss over the furniture. In minutes Ben Alden plowed a broad swath on the south side of the house, and then he crossed the road to plow west of the barn and around the other structures.

"You get this pickup out of harm's way. I'll stay and help here," Jake said.

"I want to get some saddles from the barn," she answered. "Thank heaven the horses are out of there!" Jake jogged beside her as she trotted to the barn. When she stopped inside, her brow furrowed. "Dad's stuff..." As her voice trailed away, she looked stricken.

"What do you want out of the barn?" Jake said briskly, knowing they were running out of time. Crackling and roaring, the fire was much closer. The wind was as high as ever and sparks constantly were caught in gusts, flying away to start new blazes.

"Everything," she said quietly. She gave a small shake of her shoulders. "Those saddles," she said, pointing, and Jake ran to get what she asked for. He carried out three saddles and put them in the pickup.

In minutes the blaze approached the barn.

"Get the pickup out of here," Jake shouted to her. "If you don't, you'll lose everything and the pickup, too."

She climbed in and was gone as more men came into view. Jake heard a shout and saw a fireman pointing. He turned and saw the first lick of flame curling on the barn roof. Jake swore, grabbing up a shovel.

Creating a barrier, the drive cut through between the house to the east and the barn, the garage, the bunkhouse and the sheds to the west, so firemen moved to widen the swath of wet, plowed ground between the barn and the house to try to save the house. Maggie's father plowed furrows, riding in widening strips while everyone battled the blaze.

When Jake spotted Maggie back with the firefighters, he worked his way toward her. "You could still get another carload of your belongings out of the house if you want. I'll help."

She shook her head. "No, we'll try to save the house. I'd rather—"

"Maggie, did you get the trunks out of the barn?" her father called, driving the tractor up beside them. Jake glanced at the barn and saw the whole building was burning now.

"No, I got the saddles."

"I'm getting them," her father said, sprinting toward the barn.

"Dad!" Maggie started after him, but Jake grabbed her arm.

"I'll go," he said and raced after her father who had already disappeared inside the barn.

Jake yanked down his bandanna and tied it over his nose. As he ran inside he put an arm up to shield his face, trying to hold his breath and not inhale the thick smoke. All around him, fire roared and he couldn't see through the smoke.

Then a figure loomed up before him. "Take this," Maggie's father shouted and thrust a small trunk at Jake.

"Sir, this building is going to go!"

"Get out!"

Sprinting outside, Jake set down the trunk and ran back toward the burning barn. He spotted a dark silhouette of a man only a few yards inside, but before he reached the open door, he heard a crack like a shotgun blast. A large beam fell.

The beam struck Ben Alden, knocking him down only a few feet from the door.

Two

Running toward the burning barn, Maggie screamed.

"I'll get him," Jake shouted. "You stay out."

Crouching to avoid smoke as much as possible, Jake raced inside. He groped his way until he spotted the figure lying in front of him, a burning beam across his legs. Without hesitation Jake grabbed the beam and shoved it away. He hoisted Maggie's father over his shoulder, moving blindly and praying he was headed toward the door and not deeper into the barn.

As he burst through smoke and into fresh air, he staggered and lowered her father carefully to the ground. While Jake yanked away the bandanna and gulped fresh air, Maggie knelt beside her dad.

"This man needs help," Jake yelled to one of the firefighters who ran toward them.

"Dad! I've called an ambulance."

"Are you all right?" a fireman asked Jake.

"Yeah," he nodded, coughing and still trying to get fresh air into his lungs. He moved back to allow two firemen to help her father.

Maggie thrust a bucket of water into Jake's hands and he poured it over himself, cold water drenching him, a momentary relief from the smoke and heat. "Thank you," she said, earnest blue eyes gazing at him. Her face was smudged with soot and her blond hair had come loose from the braid so that long strands fell freely around her face.

"Sure," he said and then she was gone, back kneeling beside her father while the firemen hovered over him.

With a rumble and a crack, the entire roof of the barn fell, sending flames and sparks shooting high overhead. Firefighters yelled as they worked frantically to keep the flames away from the house. Jake walked to a truck and poured a cup of water, gulping it, aware of hurting and stinging in a dozen different places. His hands felt like raw meat. Wind swirled against him and he lifted his head, realizing that it had shifted slightly.

When he went back to join the firefighters, he heard men talking about the wind, but conversation wasn't needed to tell him the wind was shifting. So far the flames had not crossed the road or flown over the swath of plowed dirt.

He glanced over his shoulder and saw an ambulance with flashing lights. Jake guessed they were getting Maggie's father into the ambulance. He hoped Ben Alden recovered.

The wind shifted, giving renewed energy to Jake

to battle the blaze that was now turning back on itself.

In another hour they had the blaze under control and the professionals took over to finish the work. On blackened ground lay the smoldering ruins of the barn, the garage and the other outbuildings. Everything was destroyed except the house.

"I think you should let a doctor look at your burns."

When he turned, Maggie stood only a few feet away. She had cleaned up and changed clothes. Now in jeans and a blue shirt, she looked cool and as sexy as ever. She had combed her hair and it hung in a thick braid over her shoulder.

"I'm all right."

"You don't look all right. I'm going to the hospital to see about my dad. Come with me to the emergency and someone will treat your burns."

Half of him wanted to get on his bike and go. The other half was drawn to her soft voice and big blue eyes and the sense that she really cared.

"Sure," he answered, feeling he was making a mistake, yet unable to resist hanging around her a little longer. "I need to move my bike from the road."

"I'll take you to get it." When she jerked her head, he saw she had brought her pickup back to the house. It was still loaded with her belongings.

"If you'd like, I can help you unload first."

She shook her head. "I want to get to town to see my dad."

They walked in silence to the pickup, and he climbed into the passenger side. Sliding behind the wheel, Maggie started the motor. In a few minutes she dropped him off at his bike, turned around and drove back to the house with him trailing behind.

Jake parked his bike, yanked on his black T-shirt and climbed into the pickup. "Want me to drive?"

"No," Maggie answered with amusement. "I'm accustomed to doing things for myself. And your hands look as if it would be painful to drive."

"I don't mind." As they drove away, he glanced out the window. "At least your house is saved."

"Thank heavens! It's bad enough to lose everything else, but our house would have been so much worse. I've been working to turn our home into a bed-and-breakfast. I'd hate to see all my efforts plus our belongings go up in flames like the barn did."

"Aren't you a little far out from any town for a bed-and-breakfast?"

As she shrugged, he shifted slightly in the seat, turning to study her, looking at flawless skin that he knew would be soft.

"I think some city people will enjoy a ranch experience and I can run the bed-and-breakfast while my dad runs the ranch. I'm going to give it a try. We have a big house, and I think I'll succeed."

"Have you always lived here?"

"Except for the two years while I was married. When I went to college, I lived at home and commuted. Where do you live?"

"First one place and then another," he answered. When she glanced at him, he suspected she didn't approve of his vagabond lifestyle.

"Dad said he's seen you in rodeos."

"I'm a saddle bronc rider."

"Dad used to do calf roping, but that was a long time ago. His health isn't as good as it used to be."

"Too bad. This fire is another burden."

"Thanks for stopping to warn us. It would have been worse if you hadn't."

"I don't know. No one could contain it until the wind changed." Jake continued to study her, wondering about her and her life. She was a beautiful woman, and he couldn't imagine her living like she did. "Don't you feel buried out here on your ranch?"

"Buried?"

"Seems like a quiet life."

She flashed him a smile, the first he had received, and it made his pulse jump. She had a dimple in her right cheek and the smile showed in her eyes, animating her face in a quick, enticing flash like the sun coming out from behind a cloud.

"It's a quiet life, and I love it that way. Where's your home now?"

"On my bike."

He received a startled glance and grinned at her. "I don't like a quiet life. I travel."

"Do you work or am I prying?"

"Pry away. I do bronc riding and I train horses. I just quit a job working with horses for a friend of mine near Fort Worth. After a while I get restless and I move on."

"Where's your family?"

"I don't have any."

"You had to have parents."

"They were killed in a fire," he answered, looking out the window and clenching his fists. He had told few people in his adult life about his family and he wondered why he had just told her.

She gave him a searching glance and then returned her attention to the road. "That's why you fought our fire so hard," she said quietly. "Dad and I wondered."

"Why would you wonder? Everyone out there fought hard."

"Not the way you did. You went after it like you wanted to put it out single-handedly." She gave him another searching glance.

"Is your little girl in school?" he asked, not caring about her answer, but wanting to get the conversation away from him and his family and fires.

"Not yet. Katy was just five last week. She'll be in kindergarten when the fall term starts.

"Where did you meet your husband?"

"Bart grew up here and we'd known each other forever. I think we married too young—too young for him, at least, and he didn't like being tied down. Particularly when Katy was born. He was here only a short time after her birth and then he was gone. Just like that, and Katy was without a father. Bart asked for the divorce."

"You can marry again," Jake said, thinking she could if she got off the ranch and met people. "You're young."

"I'm twenty-nine."

"That's young. I'm thirty-five."

"I won't marry again anytime soon," she replied after a moment's thought as if she hadn't considered the possibility before. He looked at her golden hair that looked soft as silk and wondered about her.

"So what are you really like, Maggie Langford? Is it Margaret?"

"It's Margaret and I'm really like the person I am right now. I love home and family."

He had already guessed that from watching her

during the day. He became silent, glancing at her occasionally, amazed someone else hadn't come along and married her and surprised she sounded so happy about her life on the farm.

Taking the highway, they drove into Stillwater, and uneasiness stirred in Jake. He should have hit the road instead of going into town with her. He didn't particularly want to go to the hospital. A shower and a pitcher of ice cold water would make him feel one hundred percent better. He caught a whiff of her perfume, a flower scent that went with her fresh ranch manner, and the enticing, feminine smell drove away all thoughts of leaving. He turned to watch her and found it a very pleasant pastime that made him forget his aches and his hurry to be on his way. What was it about her that drew him? And that first moment they had touched—in her clear, blue eyes he had seen that she had felt something, too.

When they reached the hospital, she told Jake to join her when he was released and then she went to see her father. Jake went to the emergency where a vivacious black-haired nurse treated his cuts and burns.

"You're new around here," she said and for the first time he really noticed her. Her big brown eyes gazed steadily at him while she cleaned a cut.

"Yep. I was driving past and saw the fire and stopped to tell the Aldens."

"Are you staying awhile?"

He glanced at her name tag and saw it was Laurie. "I haven't decided, Laurie. Anything worth staying for?" he asked, unable to resist flirting with her. She gave him a smile.

"We have all sorts of places: bars, honky-tonks, my apartment."

He laughed and looked at her fingers. No wedding or engagement ring. Evidently he could have a date if he wanted one. He thought of Maggie Langford and the thought of asking Laurie out vanished. He shifted restlessly, wishing again that he had his bike with him.

"Sounds interesting," he said, looking at her full lips and still thinking about Maggie. "Do you know if there is anyone around here now who might be going back by Ben Alden's place? I rode in with Maggie, but if I can find a ride, I won't trouble her for a ride home. My bike is at her place."

Laurie moved close against his knees and tilted his chin up to work on a cut on his temple. She paused and looked into his eyes. "If you can wait until I get off, I can take you to the Circle A ranch to get your bike," she said in a sultry voice.

"Thanks. Maybe I'll return later and take you up on that offer, but I need to get going. The fire delayed me today."

She smiled and nodded, and he didn't know if he had softened his refusal enough to keep from hurting her feelings, but he didn't want to take her out. He didn't want to think about why because it had been a long time since he'd had a date with a woman who was fun and pretty. He was ready for a night out, but this wasn't the night.

"I don't know who can take you back. You might ask if Jeff Peterson is still here. He lives out past the Alden place."

"Thanks."

Ten minutes later, Jake asked at the front desk if

anyone named Peterson was still around and was told that Jeff Peterson had left the hospital about five minutes earlier. Jake's only choices were to hitch a ride, wait for Maggie to go home or have a date with Laurie.

He asked for Ben Alden's room and rode the elevator upstairs. When he rapped lightly on the partially closed door and thrust his head into the room, Ben motioned to him. "Come in. I want to thank you. You saved my life." Ben was bandaged and propped up in bed.

Jake shrugged. "Sorry you got hurt and sorry so much of your place burned." Maggie stood across the room from him on the opposite side of her father's bed.

As Jake entered the room, Maggie watched him. He was broad-shouldered, muscular and his presence seemed to electrify the air. There was an earthy sensuality to him, yet she wondered if she thought that because he was in a tight T-shirt, covered with soot, cut and burned instead of dressed in freshly laundered clothes, looking like most other people. She suspected in freshly laundered clothes, he would never look like most other people. His height, rugged features and wild black hair would keep him from blending into a crowd. It was his riveting brown eyes that disturbed her the most. Her gaze slid down over his slim hips. His jeans rode low. She looked up, caught him watching her and blushed at the manner in which she had been studying him.

She was too conscious of his hot-blooded looks, his blunt questions. She tried to shift her thoughts, telling herself he would be out of her life as soon as she took him home tonight. He was going to set off on his bike and she wouldn't ever see him again.

"We'll build back," her father answered Jake. "Thank you for your help."

"You're welcome. How are you feeling?" Jake asked.

"Pretty good, considering," Ben answered, smiling ruefully and raising bandaged hands.

"Pretty good with burns and a broken leg," Maggie remarked dryly. "But you really did save him from being hurt much worse."

"That's good. I'm sorry about your injuries."

"I'll mend. I've mended before. Maggie tells me you've been working with horses."

"Yes, sir. I've been in Texas, working for Jeb Stuart. I'll be in a rodeo in Oklahoma City Labor Day weekend, so I wound my work up with Jeb and hit the road. I was just driving past your place when I saw the fire."

"I thought Jeb Stuart was your biggest rival in saddle bronc riding."

"He is, but he's also my best friend," Jake replied.

"Where are you going from here—except for the rodeo?"

"Dad, maybe that's private," Maggie said, glancing at Jake.

He smiled at her, holding her gaze while he answered. "No, not private at all. I don't have any plans. Just whatever comes along."

"Good. I'm laid up here and will be when I get home. How about coming to work for us until I get on my feet? I need someone badly."

Shocked, Maggie's head whipped around as she

stared at her father. They hadn't discussed hiring
Jake Reiner or anyone else. When Jake frowned, she
guessed that he didn't want to work for them and
relief washed over her. Astounded her father would
ask him without consulting her, she wondered if her
father was thinking clearly or if the pain pills had
muddled his thought processes. Their small bunkhouse for hired help had burned so they had no place
for a hired hand to live—not even in the barn. Jake
Reiner would have to stay in the house with them.
Actually he would be alone in the house with her
because Katy was at Patsy's and her father wouldn't
be coming home for another day.

"I know you've been more than a help to us so
far. A life saver, really, but I can't take care of things
for a little while. If you could just stay at the Circle
A and work until I'm able to get back to it, I'd make
it worth your while. You've got to eat, sleep and
work somewhere," he added.

Jake Reiner took a deep breath.

"Dad, Jake probably already had plans."

Her father turned his head to look at her. "Honey,
I worry about you and I know I should be home
taking care of things. Jake just left a job and he said
he's free. We need him sort of on the desperate
side." He looked at Jake. "We usually have four or
five men working for us, but for one reason or another, we don't have any now. I promise to make
working for us worthwhile for you," he repeated.

She looked into Jake's eyes and knew he didn't
want to stay. Why didn't he just say so and go!

"Dad—"

He waved his hand. "Let the man get a word in,
Maggie. I'll only be laid up for a short time and if

it gets too long for you, Jake," he said, turning his attention back to Jake, "we'll find a replacement for you. In the meantime, I could sure use your help."

Jake was still gazing into Maggie's eyes. Looking into his dark, inscrutable gaze, she held her breath.

"Yes, sir," he said quietly.

She closed her eyes and rubbed her temple. What had her father done? She was sure he wasn't thinking clearly. They would need help, but they could find someone who lived in the area and had a house or room they could go back to every night. What was she going to do with Jake Reiner?

"Thanks, Jake," Ben said, closing his eyes. "I can't tell you how relieved that makes me feel. Now I can just worry about rebuilding."

"Dad, just think about getting well," Maggie said. "I'm staying tonight at the hospital so—"

"No, you're not. I want a quiet night's sleep," her father interjected, "and Imogene is the night nurse. You know she'll take good care of me," he added and chuckled.

Maggie knew she wouldn't be needed at the hospital. For the past two years, Imogene Randle had wanted to marry her father. Now, here at the hospital, Imogene had him in her clutches, and Maggie was sure Imogene would be in his room constantly. The past twenty minutes were the longest she had been out of his room since Maggie arrived. Maggie looked at Jake again and met another curious stare. She was going to have to take him home with her and let him stay there.

Her stomach fluttered at the thought. He disturbed her and he was a stranger even though her father knew him from rodeos. Just because the guy won big belt buckles and had lots of money didn't make him safe to take into their house.

She rubbed her earlobe nervously and tried to think what she could do to change the situation. She looked at her father who was breathing deeply with his eyes closed.

"He's asleep. And he's right about Imogene. She'll check on him constantly so I guess we might as well go." Dazed by the swift turn of events, Maggie picked up her purse. "Are you ready to go home?"

The words had a strange ring to them. She knew this wasn't an ordinary man and taking him home with her was not like taking the next half dozen strangers home.

Was she really scared of him or was she scared of her own reactions to him? she wondered.

He nodded and turned to hold the door for her. Neither of them said a word as they rode down in the elevator and headed for her pickup. All the time in her mind, she kept running through the names of every hired hand they'd had or anyone else she could think of she could hire in place of Jake. Surely there was someone, and Jake had looked as if he would jump at the chance to go. Why had he let her father talk him into this?

"I know you don't want to do this. I'm sure I can find someone else," she said as she drove out of the hospital lot.

He twisted in the seat to look at her. They were still in the glow of town lights and she could see him well enough to see the flare of amusement in his eyes.

"You don't want me to work for you, do you?"

"I don't know you."

"Look, if you don't want me there, I'll go."

She shot him a look and then thought about her father. "Let me see if I can hire someone else. You really don't want to work for us, do you?"

"No. It's nothing personal. I had planned to take off work for a short time and travel, but your father needs help. More than you can give him if you're doing the cooking and taking care of your little girl. You see who you can hire. In the meantime, don't worry. I'm a safe, trustworthy person. If you'd like, you can call Jeb Stuart and get references. When we get to your house, I'll give you his number."

"Thanks. It just makes me nervous for you to move into our house when I don't know you," she admitted.

He shrugged. "It's summer. I saw a hammock in your yard—I can sleep there."

"You don't mind?"

"Nope."

She nodded and was silent and wondered what was running through his mind and if he thought that she was the silliest female he had ever encountered. He hadn't wanted to stay and work for them, yet why was he so reluctant to stay? She would call Jeb Stuart when they got home.

"When will your daughter come home?"

"I'll pick her up in the morning. I have two married sisters who live in town. They have kids, too, and all the little cousins are close."

"Nice big family," he said glancing around. "Are there any restaurants between here and your house? It just dawned on me and my stomach that I haven't eaten since last night."

"Sorry. There isn't anything unless we turn around and go back to town, but I have leftovers at home."

"That's good enough. I'd like to take a shower."

"Of course. I'm sorry about your staying in our house—"

"Forget it," he said.

They lapsed into silence again with the rumble of the pickup's engine the only noise. Jake stared into the dark night and felt caught in a trap. The father wanted him to stay, the daughter wanted him to go. And he wanted to go, dammit! Yet when he looked into the old man's eyes and then into hers, out had come an acceptance. He was getting himself tied down when he didn't want to be, in a place he didn't want to be. He was drawn to Maggie Langford and that alone made him uneasy. Most women he met were like the nurse in the emergency—flirtatious, fun and someone he could take or leave. And he always left them.

A broken leg took weeks to mend. Jake had had enough breaks to know. He didn't want to work at Maggie's ranch for weeks. And she sure as hell didn't want him to. If looks could send him flying to Mars, he would be on his way now.

He didn't mind sleeping out in the yard in the hammock. It would probably be cool and comfortable, but it was ridiculous. If he intended to harm her, staying in the yard wouldn't stop him. He was going home to eat with her and shower in her house. He glanced at her again. She was definitely easy to look at. He liked her better in shorts and a T-shirt.

They drove up to the darkened house, and she cut the engine. When he started to get out, he saw her staring at their burned field and the ruins of the garage and the barn.

"Sorry," he said, understanding too well her sense of loss and sobered by the sight of the blackened land that brought back ugly memories for him.

"It happened so fast and took so much. It'll take a long time to get things back to the way they were. Dad was after a trunk of old things that had been his father's."

"That's not as important as his life."

"I know, but he was upset and wanted to save it. I should have had you help me get those trunks out before I ever left the house the first time."

"You did the best you could."

She turned to look at him. "It's been a long day. Sorry if I'm less than hospitable. You've been good to us."

He shrugged. "Forget it." He stepped out and came around to open her door as she opened it. He held it for her and closed it. Getting some fresh clothes from his bike, he caught up with her and walked with her through the gate where she stopped abruptly.

"Oh, my!" Following her gaze, he looked at her family belongings that he had helped her move out of the house earlier. "Our friends must have moved everything back up here in front of the house."

"Where'd you put all this when you left here?"

"Across the road from the fire and friends saw me and helped unload the pickup each time. I thought I'd go back and get it tomorrow."

"I'll move it inside for you."

"Thanks, but not now. I'm exhausted and no rain

is predicted for the rest of the week. We'll do that tomorrow.''

"Sure," he said easily as they went inside. She switched on lights in a kitchen that had high ceilings and glass-fronted cabinets. Some appliances were new, and the place looked comfortable with plants, a large walnut table and yellow chintz-covered cushions.

"Do you mind giving me Jeb Stuart's phone number?" she asked. His gaze drifted down to her full lips and he wondered what it would be like to kiss her. Forget it, he told himself. The lady is definitely off-limits. Yet what was it about her that made him think of long, wet kisses and hot nights? She was Mom and apple pie, wholesome, uninterested in men at this point in her life. He shouldn't give her a second glance or thought. But something happened every time he was around her or she looked at him, something that started his pulse racing. He wondered if the smoke and fire had done something to his senses. If it had, it would be a far less disturbing discovery than to know she could have that effect on him by doing nothing more than looking up at him with those big blue eyes.

When she handed him a pen and a tablet, his fingers brushed hers. He was instantly aware of their fingers touching. Fingers. Nothing except the most casual contact. Except there was nothing casual about the effect on his system. What was it about her?

At the hospital the nurse had blatantly rubbed against him, hip against leg, her body against his shoulder, her soft breast pressing against his back and none of her contacts had done to him what the slightest brush of his fingers against Maggie's did.

Amazement warred with fear in him. No woman had ever caused such an intense reaction. He didn't want this one to.

He scribbled Jeb's number and gave the pen and tablet back.

"C'mon. I'll show you where the bathroom is and where the towels are."

Entranced by the slight sway of her hips and the faint scent of her perfume, he walked behind her through a wide hallway. Large, high-ceilinged rooms were on either side of the hallway. With paneling and beams and mahogany trim, the rooms looked livable and comfortable. The decor was chintz, patterned material and lace. Antiques sat on shelves and tables while pictures decorated the walls. The house held a cozy charm, and he could easily imagine her living in it.

"Your home is nice. This was built by your grandfather?"

"Yes, and then he married grandmother and added on to the house. When it passed to Dad, he built the family room, a bath and another bedroom. I love the old house. I've redecorated a lot of it, getting it ready to be a bed-and-breakfast."

She turned and walked down the hall and he moved beside her. "You'll have strangers in your house when you have a bed-and-breakfast."

"That'll be different," she said, then bit her lip and her cheeks flushed, and his curiosity soared about her answer.

"How'll it be different?"

The pink in her cheeks deepened. "Dad will be home then."

"He might not be here every night. And your

daughter might be gone, too. I don't think that's what you meant when you said it would be different, Maggie,'' he drawled softly, taking her arm lightly. ''How'll it be different?''

He was aware of touching her, holding her arm so lightly because he didn't want to frighten her. And he knew he was treading dangerous ground with his persistent question, yet he couldn't resist. Sparks flew between them that kept the air and his blood sizzling. He wanted to kiss her and he wanted to hear the answer to his question.

She looked up at him, wide-eyed, but in the depths of her eyes was something else, something age-old, a look from a woman to a man, and his pulse jumped.

''You probably have this effect on every woman,'' she said so quietly he had to lean closer to hear her.

''What effect?'' he asked, with his voice getting husky.

She gave a toss of her head and sparks glittered in the depths of her eyes. ''You know good and well what effect you have!'' She turned and waved her hand toward an open bedroom decorated in blue. ''You can have that bedroom to change in. There's a bathroom connected to it and there are towels and wash cloths in the bathroom cabinet. Help yourself. I'll be downstairs.'' Her words were rushed together.

If he wasn't filthy, sweaty, burned and blistered from the fire he would have pursued their conversation, but right now he wanted a shower before he got one inch closer to her and delved into her remarks that set his heart racing.

She hurried to the stairs and turned to look at him. ''Would you like a salad and cold chicken and a baked potato?''

"That sounds great. I'll be down soon."

She nodded and disappeared and he wiped his hot brow as he turned to enter a large bedroom with a bright blue-and-white quilt on the brass bed. In minutes he was in the shower and he wondered if she was talking to Jeb for a reference.

Downstairs, Maggie doodled on the pad while she listened to Jeb Stuart. Then her hand became still and she turned to look at the empty doorway while she listened, and her heart started drumming while her ideas about Jake took another sharp turn.

Three

Maggie listened to the deep voice on the phone tell her how reliable Jake was. Jeb told her in detail how Jake had saved his life in Colombia when they had been in the Airborne and on a rescue mission. Closing her eyes, she could visualize the image again of Jake running into the burning barn and then just minutes later, emerging with her father slung over his shoulder. So he was reliable and a wonderful person and she had insulted him and she was being ridiculous.

"Thank you," she said quietly, only a portion of her uneasiness erased. She replaced the receiver and stared out the window at the blackened field. She didn't want Jake working for them, but it was that disturbing electricity she experienced every time she was around him that worried her. She didn't remember feeling that way around Bart and she had been in love with him and had married him.

She gave a slight shake of her shoulders. She and Jake had already discussed the situation. She would hire someone else, and he would go. He didn't want to be tied down here anyway.

She got out the cold chicken and swiftly set the table, putting potatoes in the microwave oven to bake, then getting out the loaf of homemade bread that was only half eaten. She sliced tomatoes and set them on the table.

"What a picture," Jake drawled, and she spun around. He stood in the doorway with his hair slicked back, giving him an entirely different appearance, revealing his prominent cheekbones more sharply. He had changed to a white T-shirt and wore jeans and his boots, a sight that made her pulse skip.

"Picture?"

"A pretty woman, scrumptious chicken and an old-fashioned kitchen."

"I wouldn't think those would be the things that appeal to you. You sound like you like life in the fast lane."

He shrugged and strolled into the room, dark gaze on her, and a faint smile curving his mouth. "I like all of those things—pretty women, good food—I guess I don't care one way or other about kitchens. Since I haven't eaten for over twenty-four hours now, that food looks like a feast."

"I'll pour water and we'll eat."

As she reached into the cabinet, his hand brushed hers and he took a glass from her. She turned and he was right beside her, brushing against her shoulder. "I'll get the drinks."

"If you look in the back in the bottom of the fridge, you'll probably find a cold beer. Dad has one now and then."

"Thanks, but I don't drink beer." Jake's brow arched. "I surprised you, didn't I?"

As heat flushed her cheeks, she realized she had to stop judging him by his appearance. "You've surprised me all day," she admitted.

"Good," he said in a tone of voice that changed subtly and made her tingle. "Life is interesting when it holds surprises."

"It depends on the surprises. The fire today was one heck of a surprise."

"It was a shock and a bad one. That isn't what I'm talking about, Maggie."

"I'll drink ice water," she said, trying to get back on an impersonal level. Amusement flashed in his dark eyes before he headed to the refrigerator. She wondered if she would ever forget him moving around their house. What was it about him that carried that air of wild recklessness? He hadn't done anything that had been out of line, yet she had the feeling he was not only capable of wildness, but that was his usual mode. She glanced out the window at the big Harley parked outside.

Setting two glasses of water on the table, he held a chair for her and she sat down. "Thanks."

He sat facing her and as she passed the chicken to him, the phone rang. She got up to answer it, motioning him to go ahead.

It was the insurance adjustor, and she made an appointment for the next morning, the first Wednesday in August. She sat down to eat when the phone rang again.

"Go ahead and eat," she said as she answered to talk to a friend.

While she was on the phone, someone drove up and knocked at the back door. Jake opened it for Melody Caldwell, one of Maggie's friends. Maggie saw that Melody carried a large casserole dish.

Maggie watched while Jake flirted with Melody and Melody flirted back. Divorced, Melody lived in town. She and Maggie had known each other since they were five and Maggie knew Melody would be in no hurry to go home. She would be fascinated with Jake.

Maggie hung up. "Hi, Melody. Thanks for the food. I see you two met." She heard an engine and glanced out to see a ranch neighbor drive up. Dressed in jeans and matching Western shirts, looking more like brother and sister than husband and wife with their red hair, Ollie and Pru Morgan climbed out of their truck and crossed the porch with food in hand. Within the hour two more neighbors arrived. After supper, all the friends helped Maggie and Jake move her things back inside the house.

It was half past ten when the last guest left. Maggie was aware of Jake standing beside her on the porch as her neighbors drove away.

"You have a lot of friends."

"I've lived here all my life and so have my parents and my grandparents before them."

Jake sat down on the wooden steps. "It's cool and nice out here now. Sit down a minute."

"I miss Katy being here."

"You just talked to her a little while ago."

"I know. She likes to stay with her cousins, and it's good for them to grow up friends, but I miss her.

Patsy has two girls, Ella who is seven and Tina who is five.''

Aware of him only a few feet away, Maggie sat down on the steps. Beside her, he stretched his long legs out in front of him. The night was cool and quiet with only the chirp of crickets and the far-off sound of a bullfrog.

"You have enough food from your friends to last the rest of the week," Jake said.

"They've all been nice."

"Yeah. It's great. What would you like me to do in the morning?"

"I guess you can take over Dad's chores. Because of the drought, he's having to feed the cattle and horses. He checks on their water. We have a stallion, Red Rogue—Dad just calls him Rogue. He's wild so be careful of him. He's penned up by himself in the northeast pasture. Dad is trying to sell him, we have an ad running, but so far, no buyers." She raised her head. "I can smell the burned land."

"Yep, but it won't last long and several of the men said in the seven-day forecast, rain is predicted. First thing you know, it'll all green up again."

"Thank goodness the fire didn't cross the lane and we have our house and trees left in the yard."

While fireflies flitted over the fenced yard, Maggie and Jake sat in an easy silence, and she was amazed he wanted to just sit and enjoy the evening. He was only a few feet from her, and she was very conscious of him.

"You want to have a bed-and-breakfast and you want your little girl to grow up here. What else do you want from life?"

"That's about all. I'm happy here with my dad

and Katy. This is a good life.'' She glanced around. Jake leaned back on his elbows, almost reclining on the steps with his legs in front of him. He watched her, but she could no longer see the expression in his eyes.

"What do you want, Jake?"

"I want to see parts of the world I haven't already seen. I want to save my money and travel around the world."

"Your life is hard for me to imagine," she said. "I've never been out of Oklahoma."

"No kidding!" She saw a flash of his white teeth. "Maybe one day you should let your sister keep Katy and get on my bike with me and let me take you across the state line to Texas."

She smiled. "Maybe someday I'll go somewhere. Tonight I'm going to bed. I'm exhausted." She stood. "If you'd like, you can sleep upstairs. I'm sorry I wasn't hospitable.

He stood and faced her, shaking his head. "Forget it. That hammock looks inviting, and I like it out here under the stars. I haven't slept outside in a long time. I'll come in and shower in the morning."

"Come get a pillow. You won't need a blanket."

He held the door and they went inside. She left him in the kitchen while she went upstairs and got a sheet and a pillow and brought them back to him. His hands brushed hers as he took the items from her.

"See you in the morning," he drawled. The words should have been a brief parting that she barely noticed, but they weren't. In his husky, soft voice, they were like a caress of his fingers. His eyes held hers extra heartbeats while the silence between them stretched, and she was lost in his gaze.

"Sure," she whispered.

He turned and crossed the room to the door where he paused and glanced over his shoulder at her. "You can lock up. I won't need to come back inside until morning."

She shrugged, embarrassed she had made it so clear that she didn't trust him and didn't want him in her home. "That's all right. We don't always lock up anyway."

"You don't lock your door, Maggie Langford, but you keep your heart locked away," he said, raising an eyebrow. Before she could answer, he was gone, closing the door behind him.

Startled by his statement, she stared at the door. "I need to keep it locked away when you're around," she replied softly. What was it about him that was so blatantly sexy?

She switched off the lights and went upstairs to bed. Before she turned on the lights in her bedroom, she walked to the window. The hammock was below, and she could easily see him stretched out on it. He had shed his T-shirt and boots and wore only his jeans. He lay with his hands behind his head and she wondered if he could see her at the window. She pulled the shade and moved away to turn on a bed-side lamp.

She was exhausted, yet she wasn't certain she would sleep. She hated to think of all the work that lay ahead of them, just trying to restore what burned. Thank heavens they had insurance that would carry them through this. But insurance wouldn't replace trees.

She got ready for bed, slipping into an oversize T-shirt. When she switched off the lights and climbed into bed, she was still aware of Jake sleeping down in the yard. He was outside the house, but in her thoughts to a degree that disturbed her.

He flirted a little, but hadn't come on strong, so why was she having this volatile reaction to him? She fell asleep thinking about him.

In the cool night Jake watched the leaves flutter with the breeze. In spite of the smell of charred land, it was cool and peaceful outside. His burns ached and the hammock wasn't particularly comfortable because of blisters and cuts across his back and shoulders, but he was tired and he tried to shut his mind to his aches. Instead he thought about Maggie with her door unlocked, yet she was shut away from the world. She hadn't ever left the state and she didn't date. What was she hiding from? Or maybe it wasn't hiding, but just rooted to this place like the big trees around him.

The thought of always staying in one place sounded like prison to him. She was a beautiful woman and it seemed a waste. He was sure she was a good daughter and a good mother, but she was missing out on a big chunk of life.

He gave a small cynical laugh in the darkness. She was probably thinking just the same about him and feeling he was missing out on life because he didn't have a home and roots and family. She certainly had a lot of friends who had come to her aid. If his bike burned up who would even know? But that's the way he liked to live.

He wondered if he could coax her out dancing one

night. He thought about how skittish she was around him and doubted if he could. What would it be like to kiss her?

"You'll never know, buddy," he said to himself in the dark and looked at the bedroom where he had seen her standing at the window. She was aware of him, he knew that.

Wishing for a bed with cool sheets where he could sleep on his stomach and get the pressure off his blisters and cuts, he shifted and tried to get comfortable.

He watched the leaves flutter and sway and then he was asleep and the next conscious thing he knew was the ring of a phone.

Instantly awake and aware of where he was, he opened his eyes and stared into the darkness. He listened to two more rings and looked up at Maggie's darkened room. Someone was calling her in the middle of the night. Couldn't she hear the phone? He could hear it and he was outside the house.

He started to close his eyes and forget it, but he thought about her little girl. Sprinting to the back door, he half expected to find himself locked out. The door came open and he hit the light switch and crossed the kitchen to answer the phone.

There was a second's pause before a female voice spoke. "You must be Jake. I'm Patsy, Maggie's sister. I need to speak to her."

"I don't know why she didn't answer. I'll go see," he said, wondering what had happened to her.

"She's a very sound sleeper. You'll probably have to wake her, Jake. It's Dad. He's had a heart attack."

"On, damn. Sorry. I'll get her."

Jake swore softly to himself as he put down the

receiver. Maggie and her father had had enough trouble with the fire. They didn't need any more calamities. He took the stairs two at a time and turned toward the room where he had seen her.

Her door was closed, and he knocked and called. "Maggie!"

Nothing.

How soundly did the woman sleep? This was like someone unconscious. He opened the door and stepped inside. "Maggie!"

She was sprawled on the bed, covers kicked away while a ceiling fan slowly revolved. She wore a T-shirt that was high around her thighs and her long legs were bare. As he crossed the room to shake her shoulder, Jake drew a deep breath. She had taken down her braid and long, golden hair spilled over her and the pillow. Swiftly he imagined her without the T-shirt as he touched her shoulder.

She was soft and warm and it was an effort to keep his mind on the emergency. He couldn't resist running his fingers through strands of her hair. It was like silk, sliding over his hand. "Maggie, wake up!" His voice was husky as he shook her more forcefully. "Maggie!"

"Mmm," she said and rolled over, burying her face in the pillow. Moonlight spilled over her shapely curves. The T-shirt had ridden higher and the lush curve of her bottom clad in a wisp of lace was revealed. Drawing a deep breath, he felt on fire. He turned on a light, saw the bedside phone and shook her shoulder again.

Stirring, she rolled over again and looked up at him, and Jake felt as if something had knocked the breath from his lungs. The long blond hair fell over her shoulders and the T-shirt had molded to her full breasts. Wordlessly he handed her the phone.

Maggie swung her legs over the side of the bed and sat up, shaking the golden cascade of her hair away from her face and tugging down the T-shirt as she held the receiver and listened.

As if snapped out of a dream, she suddenly raised her chin and stood. "I'll be there as quickly as I can," she said solemnly.

As soon as she replaced the receiver, Jake asked, "How is he?"

"Stable."

"Get dressed. I'll drive you to town."

"You don't need to," she said, combing her hands through her hair.

"I don't mind. I'll hang up the phone downstairs. Give me your keys, and I'll bring the pickup to the back gate."

She motioned. "My keys are on the dresser."

As Jake crossed the room to pick them up, he glanced in the mirror and saw her head for her bathroom. The T-shirt covered her bottom, but it clung and he watched the sway of her hips. When he turned and left, he wondered how long it would take him to forget the last few minutes and how she had looked waking up in bed.

In five minutes, dressed in jeans and a blue shirt, her hair tied behind her head with a strip of blue ribbon, she came running out of the house and climbed into the pickup beside him.

"This is his second heart attack," she said tensely.

"How long ago was the other one?"

"Three years ago. I wonder if the fire brought this on."

They lapsed into silence and Jake drove fast, knowing she was worried and wanted to get there as quickly as possible.

At the hospital, he stopped in front and reached across her to open the door. "Go on inside. I'll be up after I park," he said, opening her door.

She slid out and vanished through wide glass doors. He parked and went inside, going to the floor where her father was. He stopped at the nurse's desk and asked about her dad and learned that Ben had had a mild attack and was stable, but he had been moved to intensive care.

For the first time Jake thought about what this would mean for him and realized he might be working longer at their ranch than he had planned. He strolled down the hall and saw Maggie with two other women. He recognized her sister Patsy.

"Maggie, I'll be in the waiting room."

All three women turned to look at him. He could see little resemblance between them except two of them were blond. Patsy was the brunette he had seen at the ranch. Maggie was the tallest.

"Jake, this is my sister Patsy Loomis and my other sister, Olivia Sommersby."

"Hi. Sorry about your father."

They said hello and thanked him for his concern and then he went back to the empty waiting room. Jake sat down, stretched out his legs, and closed his eyes.

The next thing he knew someone was waking him. He came to his feet to face Maggie.

"Sorry. It's after three in the morning. I'm ready to go home now. The doctor said Dad's doing better and since he was right here in the hospital, they realized at once what was happening and could do something for him immediately. The doctor's given me a lot of hope.''

"Good.'' They fell into step as they walked outside. In the parking lot, Jake took Maggie's arm and led her toward the pickup.

"I guess we got about an hour's sleep before they called.'' She ran her fingers across her forehead.

"Did your sisters go home?''

"Yes, long before now.''

He held the door of the pickup for her and went around to slide behind the wheel. Going home they were silent again and he suspected her nerves were frayed. When they reached the house, he parked at the gate and got out, coming around to open the door. He went inside with her. "Want something cold to drink?'' he asked, as if he were the host and she the guest.

She nodded. "Just a glass of tea. I know I won't sleep, but I feel exhausted.'' She ran her hands over her forehead. "I hope nothing else happens.''

Wrung-out and exhausted, Maggie still worried about her father. The doctor had reassured her of the prognosis, but she knew this would change the future. "Dad won't be able to work like he always has,'' she said, barely aware of Jake as he poured two glasses of iced tea. Jake brought one drink to her and pulled out a kitchen chair. "Come sit down.''

With her thoughts still on her father and the changes they would have to make now in the ranch routine, she sat down and sipped the cold drink. Jake pulled another chair from the table. He moved it around to her side. "Turn around in your chair.''

He motioned, and she realized he intended to give her a back rub and the notion was welcome. She turned her back to him and wondered how he had gone so fast from a total stranger to someone living in their house, driving her pickup and now, giving her a back rub. His hands were strong and steady as he rubbed her shoulders and moved to her neck, his hand rotating with just the right amount of pressure to make her close her eyes. She could feel the tension leave her body.

"Relax," he said quietly. "You're tense—no surprise. Anybody would be tense after what you went through today."

"What makes you tense, Jake?" she asked, slanting him a look, curious about him and trying to get her thoughts off the problems ahead of her.

"Fire, for one thing. Coming out of the chute on a bucking bronc makes me a little tense."

"And that's probably all," she answered with amusement. "No cares, no responsibilities, no ties."

"No pain. Look at you now, tied up in knots over someone you love, frazzled today over the home you love."

"It's worth it," she said solemnly, taken aback by his statement. His gaze slid past her, and she knew he was thinking about someone else or somewhere else.

"Not when the deep hurts come. Not when people die," he said solemnly, and she wondered whether his whole family had perished in the fire, but she didn't want to ask. He focused on her again, his eyes searching. "I've told you things today that I haven't told people who've known me for years. You get to someone easily, Maggie. You must know lots of secrets."

She turned away. "I could say the same about you, Jake. This morning we were total strangers. Now you're living in my house. Your hands are on me now."

For just an instant, his hands stilled and then he continued. They both were silent and she wondered what ran through his thoughts.

His hand kneaded her back between her shoulder blades, then he began massaging upward and out in slow, steady strokes.

"Now I know why cats purr. This is helping me relax."

"Good," he said, close to her ear. He began to take down her thick braid, the tugs to her scalp sensuous as he pulled gently. Slowly he combed his fingers through the long strands.

"You have beautiful hair," he said softly, and a tingle fluttered in her.

"Thanks." Her curiosity about him was only increasing. "Jake, don't you ever want to have a family of your own? Just someday in the far distant future? Don't you want to ever love and be loved?"

He worked his way across her back and down. "I don't want to be tied down." His voice was harsh, and she sensed he didn't want to talk about losing his family in a fire. "Besides, there's plenty of loving out there. I didn't say I don't like that," he added on a lighter note.

"So there are girlfriends," she said, switching to the present.

"Nope. None at present." This time his voice was lighter and his answer had come quickly.

"Why do I find that incredibly hard to believe?" she asked dryly, and he chuckled.

"No more difficult than for me to believe there are no men in your life."

"Well, there sure aren't any. The most eligible bachelor in this county is Weldon Higgens. He lives next door and doesn't like us at all. You didn't see Weldon fighting that fire today even though it could have burned across our land and onto his."

"Has he ever asked you out?"

"Right after I got divorced and moved back here."

"Did you go out with him?"

She had her eyes closed, lost in the back rub and barely aware of Jake's questions. His hands were working their magic and she was aware of his legs stretched out on either side of her. He was sitting close behind her and his voice was deep and husky in her ears.

"No, I didn't. I don't like the way he looks at me." She paused, realizing what she had just told Jake. "There, I did it again—telling you something I've never told anyone else. You have a way with people, too, Jake." Her voice had slurred, and the tension had left her. She could feel the exhaustion setting in, along with relief that her father had a good prognosis, that the fire was out and that the house hadn't burned.

"The massage feels so good," she said languidly. "I can relax now."

"If you want to go to bed, I'll give you a massage until you go to sleep. I promise to tiptoe out and leave you alone."

Shaking her hair away from her face, she turned

to look at him, amusement tugging at the corners of her mouth. "I think that would be pushing things a bit," she said. "And I don't think I trust you quite that much."

While he gazed at her solemnly, his hands combed through her hair slowly. Drawing a swift breath, she realized it might have been a mistake to turn and face him because awareness, sexual and hot, flared like spontaneous combustion.

They were only inches apart. He sat with his legs spread on either side of her chair, his hands slowly tugging through the long strands of her hair in touches that seemed more intimate than the back rub. His eyes were black pools enveloping her, carrying a midnight magic.

"Ah, Maggie, live a little. Just a little," he coaxed softly, his gaze lowering to her mouth.

Her pulse drummed. Wisdom said move away from him, yet she couldn't move. She was as immobile and steady as everything else about her life. What would it hurt if they kissed? Just one kiss. Her pulse raced because she wanted his kiss. She wanted to do this while she had the chance. This one moment she wanted to break free from the everyday constraints of her routine ranch life.

He looked at her mouth and then into her eyes, and she saw his intent before his gaze slipped to her lips again. When he leaned closer, her heart thudded, and, knowing what she wanted, she slid her hand to the back of his neck. His skin was smooth and warm, coarse strands of hair brushing the back of her hand lightly.

When she touched him, his gaze flew to meet hers again with a questioning stare. She was certain he hadn't expected her to put her hand on the back of his neck. Was she making him bolder?

At the moment she didn't care. She wanted him to kiss her. She wanted to taste and touch and be kissed by this wild, reckless cowboy who was so many things she was not. He was irresistible. Scary. Thrilling.

She closed her eyes and raised her mouth in anticipation.

He leaned closer until his mouth covered hers firmly. With that first touch, desire exploded in her. Moaning softly, she pulled his head closer.

When his tongue slid into her mouth, she was lost in a dizzying spiral of sensation as she kissed him back, her tongue in a delicious duel that made her blood roar.

His hands slid down to her waist and he moved her, lifting her easily off the chair and into his lap. She didn't care. How long—years—since she had been held and kissed by a man?

She had never known a kiss like this that made her toes curl and her heart pound and her blood heat to melted fire.

She moaned again, dimly hearing her own voice, aware of the warmth and textures of him, the soapy clean scent tinged faintly with the scents of salve and antiseptic and his cotton T-shirt. When her hand slid across his shoulder over the ridges and roughness beneath his T-shirt, she remembered his burns and cuts.

"Your back!" she whispered, afraid she had hurt him, startled when she touched his injuries.

He made a sound deep in his throat and tightened his arm around her and stopped any more words, leaning over her and kissing her hard. Sliding her arm around his neck, she forgot his injuries. Desire burned in her, need throbbing with each heartbeat.

Caution and consequences no longer mattered. At the moment she just wanted his kisses and wanted him never to stop. She returned them wildly, passionately, letting go of all else until deeper needs began to burn into her awareness, and she knew she had to stop before passion blazed beyond control.

Dazed by his kisses, aroused by his reactions, she pushed against him. Instantly he raised his head and looked into her eyes.

"Damn, Maggie," he whispered, and he sounded shaken.

She was surprised by his reaction, but she understood it because that was the way she felt. Her world had tilted, changed, and she knew she wasn't going to forget his kisses any faster than she would forget the fire that burned their land and barn.

She was still in his lap, her hands on his chest now. She could feel his racing heart and knew she had stirred him. When she slid off his lap and stood, he came to his feet at once, his hands resting on her waist as he stood close and looked down at her.

"Where do we go from here?" he asked, solemnly, and her heart thudded again.

Four

"We go back to the way we were before," she whispered, knowing she should sound more forceful. "Your life is that hog you ride and mine is this home and family. There's a chasm between us that's enormous. You can't cross over to my side and I can't cross over to yours."

He brushed her cheek with his fingers. "Earnest Maggie. A few kisses won't change our lives."

"Not your life," she said quietly. "I usually get up in another hour—I won't today, but morning will come all too soon. I'm going to bed, Jake. Thanks for taking me to town. You were a help."

"Go on to bed. I'll turn out the lights."

She nodded and left him, feeling his gaze on her as she walked out of the room. His words taunted her, *"A few kisses won't change our lives."* His kiss had been devastating. Was she that lonely and starved for loving? Or was there some special chemistry? The thought that there might be something special in Jake scared her because she suspected that was the truth. She didn't want a man like Jake to sweep into her life with the force of a whirlwind and steal her heart because he would be gone as swiftly as wild storm winds.

She tingled all over from being in his arms. "Forget him," she whispered to herself, glancing over her shoulder. Light spilled from the open kitchen door into the darkened hallway. As she watched, the light went off.

Upstairs in her room, she changed swiftly and switched off the lights in her room. Then she was unable to resist walking to the window. Quietly she raised the shade. He was stretched in the hammock again, his chest and feet bare, and she remembered what it was like to be held tightly in his strong arms against his solid chest.

She turned away and climbed into bed, staring into the darkness while all the events of the day ran through her mind—the first glimpse of the fire, Jake beating at the flames, Jake running into the barn and bringing out her father, visiting her dad in the hospital, sitting on the steps in the cool evening with Jake, being in his arms and kissing him. That set her pulse racing again and she wondered if she would sleep at all.

"Why did you come here, Jake?" she whispered in the darkness, but then guilt swamped her because he had bravely come to warn them of the fire.

Just keep a distance from him, she decided. And find another hired hand soon.

* * *

The first light of dawn woke Jake. He stretched, seeing the sun was still below the horizon. As he headed for the house, the tempting aroma of coffee and bacon assailed him.

He opened the back door to see Maggie with her back to him at the stove. She wore faded cutoffs, a red T-shirt and sneakers. Her hair was braided and hung down her back. He stood watching her a moment, enjoying the sight of her and remembering the silky feel of her hair over his hands.

"Good morning," he said quietly, fighting the temptation to cross the room and put his arms around her.

Glancing over her shoulder, she flashed a smile at him. "Hey, there. I thought since you didn't get to eat at all yesterday until last night that you might like bacon and eggs for breakfast."

"It's mouthwatering tempting," he drawled, thinking about her instead of breakfast.

Her eyes widened slightly, and that electric current snapped between them. She turned back to cook, but not before he had seen her cheeks flood with pink.

"How can I help?" he asked.

"You can fix the toast, pour the coffee," she answered, glancing over her shoulder at him.

"Sure. I'm going to wash up first," he said, crossing the room and heading for the stairs.

When he returned, he got toast and poured himself a cup of steaming black coffee, all the while intensely aware of her moving around him. Their conversation was light, although he barely thought about what he was saying because he was too conscious of her.

He inhaled, studying her when he thought she was

unaware of his scrutiny. Why was he having this intense reaction to her? He'd been around pretty women all his adult life and had never experienced such electric feelings. Her kiss last night—with another deep intake of breath he stopped that train of thought. What was worrisome, he had been having these feelings even before they had ever kissed.

Over fluffy scrambled eggs and crisp toast, he sat across the table from her and listened to her outline their day. "After I check on Dad, I'll pick up Katy. If they move Dad out of intensive care today, I'll take her to see him. We have to get some things and then I'll be back home. I also have an appointment with the insurance adjustor later today."

"And while you're gone, what do you need done here?"

"The animals need to be checked on first. Besides the pickup, we have an old truck. You can drive it. I'll draw you a map of the ranch. When you get a chance, will you please rebuild the little stretch of fence around our yard?"

"Sure."

"Katy knows to stay inside the fence so I'd like it replaced as quickly as possible. It's scary that the fire got that close to the house. It got part of the fence and the tree where her swing is."

"But that's all. At least your house and the rest of the fence and the trees close to the house are all right."

"I know and I'm grateful."

"Breakfast was delicious. Is this what you eat every morning?" She smiled and his pulse jumped a notch. He fought the impulse to reach across the table and touch the corner of her mouth.

"No, I don't. Dad and Katy need fruit so we have cereal and fruit. Tomorrow morning we'll probably be back to the usual."

"Thanks for cooking something special for me this morning," he said softly and received another wide-eyed look. "I still can't believe you're not dating."

"It's the absolute truth," she said smiling. "What's hard to believe is that you're not."

"Why don't we change that a little? If your dad is all right, let me take you dancing Saturday night."

She shot him a look and then studied her orange juice, running her slender fingers along the glass. As silence stretched between them, he caught her hand in his, running his thumb over her smooth, soft skin.

"I don't think we should," she said.

"Oh, hell, Maggie, it's just an evening out. We're not going to get serious. How much time have you taken for yourself this past year? Not much, I'll bet. It's no big deal. Just think about it and see how your dad is." He pushed back his chair a fraction and stretched out his legs. "Now after feeding and watering your animals, what do you want me to do?"

She caught her lower lip with small, white teeth and his attention focused on her rosy mouth. He wanted to kiss her again. He had said their kiss had been no big deal, but he had been wrong and he knew it.

With his mind more on her than on what she was saying, they went over chores and then she shooed him away as she began to clean the kitchen.

In minutes, outside in warm sunshine, Jake stood looking at Ben's tractor. It was corroded with rust. The engine looked as if it needed a complete overhaul. The dilapidated flatbed truck was in the same condition.

Jake roamed around, finding frayed rope and broken tools. He wondered about Ben's health and if Maggie knew her father had been letting the place go to ruin. The more Jake saw, the more his spirits sank. Maggie needed help and a lot of it.

He could feel his freedom slipping away. He wanted to put a thousand miles between Maggie and him. He didn't want to have such intense feelings for a woman.

He looked at a pile of charred boards from the barn and kicked a board, sending up a puff of soot. "Dammit," he swore.

He climbed into the flatbed truck Maggie had told him to use and looked at the sketch of the ranch she had given him. The horses had been turned out yesterday during the fire and Maggie said he would find them near a pond on the far north section of the ranch, except for the unmanageable stallion that was kept in a fenced pasture to the northeast.

Familiarizing himself with the ranch, he explored the Circle A. Later, as he stood looking at the half-dozen horses, he realized Maggie's dad knew horses and had some very fine animals. Two mares approached him, and he knew they expected to be fed. He talked quietly to them, finally running his hands over a sleek bay. Maggie might want a bed-and-breakfast so her father wouldn't have to work so hard, but right now they had a good start on a horse ranch.

Jake found their cattle and it looked as though all the animals had made it through the fire. That left him with only one more occupant to check on.

He arrived at the fenced-in pasture located on the northeastern part of the ranch. There, Jake stopped the truck and climbed out, easing the door closed. The sorrel was off in the distance, cropping grass and seemingly not interested in Jake. The horse was a magnificent animal and Jake wondered why he was such a hellion.

Moving quietly, Jake opened the gate, then drove into the pasture to the stock tank. Carefully, with an eye on the horse, Jake checked the float in the tank. He glanced at the stallion that stood a couple of hundred yards away with ears now cocked forward.

"You're curious about me, aren't you, Red Rogue?" Jake said quietly, turning his back and walking away to get a rope from the bed of the truck. He glanced over his shoulder at the stallion. The horse had moved closer, but stopped when Jake looked at him. Jake turned his back and started knotting the rope.

By the end of an hour, he knew the stallion was close behind him. Without looking back, Jake stopped working on the rope and walked over to his truck. There, he glanced back to see the horse watching him, only yards away.

"See you tomorrow, Rogue." Jake said quietly, certain the horse wasn't the rogue that Maggie and her father thought he was.

That afternoon while he washed soot off tools, Jake heard the pickup returning. When Maggie parked, Katy and their dog jumped out. Katy looked at Jake and ran toward the house. He watched her pigtails fly, and then his gaze shifted to Maggie who had her arms filled with sacks of groceries. He dropped what he was repairing and wiped his hands on a rag, then hurried to help her.

"How's your dad?" he asked Maggie as he passed her and went to retrieve the remaining bags in the back of the truck.

"Much better," Maggie said, stopping to wait for him. "They've moved him from intensive care and Katy could see him briefly."

"Good," Jake said, catching up with her. He opened the screen door and waited for her to enter. They set down sacks of groceries and Maggie began to put things away.

"I talked to Sheriff Alvarez. The fire was arson. It was deliberately set."

Startled, Jake paused in emptying a sack. "Who do they think did it? It was too far from the highway to have been a tossed cigarette."

"He said it was probably kids. The fire was set by sparklers. With this drought there is a burn ban that covers almost all of the state so anyone shooting any kind of fireworks is in violation of the law. The dry grass caught on fire."

"Kids out with sparklers during the morning?" Jake asked doubtfully.

Maggie moved around the kitchen putting away groceries. "Who else would be out with sparklers?"

Followed by the dog, Katy sidled into the kitchen and when Jake glanced her way, he smiled.

"Hi, Katy. How are you?"

Looking wide-eyed, she scooted near her mother.

"Katy, answer Mr. Reiner," Maggie prodded gently.

"Fine," she said, tugging on Maggie's cutoffs.

When Maggie leaned down, Katy whispered that

she would like a banana. Maggie gave her one, and she dashed outside.

"I must frighten her," Jake said.

"She's just not accustomed to strangers," Maggie replied. "We see the same people all the time. She's shy around most men."

"I saw your stock this morning. You have a fine herd of horses."

Maggie nodded. "That's Dad's doing. He was interested in raising horses, but then he decided he didn't want to."

"I saw Red Rogue. You said you have an ad running to sell him. Cancel it. Let me work with him. I'll either buy him myself or find a buyer."

"Let me tell you about that horse," she said, pausing with a head of lettuce in her hand. "He's a killer. He's never been ridden more than a few minutes and watch out because he'll go for you. He bites, he kicks, and he stomps when the mares are in season. We've had three hired hands who refused to even feed him. Dad doesn't like him, either, and he usually does great with all the animals."

Jake thought about the horse trailing along behind him today. "Just cancel the ad. I think he can be gentled. I might buy him."

Maggie laughed, her dimple showing. "What—and run him along behind your Harley?"

With a flash of white teeth, Jake grinned. "I own some horses and a pickup. I keep them at Jeb Stuart's place."

"Well, you can't want our stallion."

"Yes, I do."

Placing one hand on her hip, she tilted her head

to study him. "Maybe you're as stubborn as that horse. Or maybe you just like a challenge."

"Oh, I like a challenge, Maggie," Jake drawled, his voice dropping meaningfully. She was a threat to his peace of mind, and he knew he was a threat to hers. He was certain he was the kind of man she wouldn't want to get involved with.

Yet even so, he was irresistibly drawn to her. He moved closer to her, placing his hand on her hip. Her blue eyes widened, the color deepening. He rested his other hand against her throat. "Your pulse is racing."

"It doesn't matter. You keep your distance," she whispered, her gaze dropping to his mouth, and his pulse jumped another notch.

"Whatever the lady wants," he said quietly, knowing she was right. His heart pounded, drowning out other noises, and he strode across the kitchen, leaving her to put away the groceries. He had to get out of the kitchen, away from her or she would end up in his arms. And he had a feeling that if he had pulled her into his embrace and kissed her, she would have kissed him back as she had last night.

They were danger and disaster to each other so why couldn't he keep his distance? Why was his pulse roaring and his blood hot as fire? He strode across the yard and saw Katy standing by her burned swing that now was charred ruins on the ground. She was watching him and she looked frightened. He smiled as sweetly as he could. He didn't know anything about little girls. Jeb Stuart, where Jake had recently worked, had a three-year-old, but Jake had hardly ever been around her.

He walked over to Katy and she looked ready to

run. He touched the charred ruins of the swing with his toe. "Did you lose your swing in the fire?"

She nodded.

"Well, I can build you a new swing. We'll have to find another big tree to put it on. Okay?"

She nodded, and he turned to walk away, feeling she was too terrified to talk to him even a little. He glanced over his shoulder once and she was still watching him. He waved and went on his way without looking back again.

Inside the kitchen, Maggie had watched the encounter. She walked to the door. "Stay inside the fence where I can see you, Katy."

Her daughter nodded and Maggie let her gaze shift to watch Jake's long-legged stride, remembering him standing so close with his hand on her hip. She should have moved away, but she couldn't.

Late that night, after she had driven into town to the hospital and Katy was fast asleep in her bed, Maggie sat outside in the cool darkness with Jake, listening to him talk about rodeos and horses and places he'd been. For the second time that day, she thought how she should stay away from him. Do anything to keep space between her and this dangerous man who was moving swiftly into every nook and cranny of her life. But she couldn't.

Jake sat beside her on a lawn chair, his hands on his knees, leaning forward, his voice a deep rumble in the quiet night. "You know about me now, Maggie. What about you?"

Startled out of her deep thoughts, she sighed and said, "Oh, I've led a most ordinary life. Grew up here, married a local boy, had a little girl, divorced and live here now at my dad's. I haven't traveled other places, haven't seen much, but I'm happy here.''

"How long did you say you were married?"

"Two years. My husband said he was chained by marriage, as if every day another rope was tying him to this place until he wouldn't be able to move or think. Since your home is your bike, you must understand that, but I don't. I need roots and history and family."

"You love, you get hurt," Jake said gruffly, and she turned to look at him. He was staring off in the distance with his profile to her, a muscle working in his jaw.

"Who hurt you, Jake? Were you married?"

"No," he said, turning to look at her, "but if you love, sooner or later you'll hurt."

"It's worth hurting to know love," she said, wondering what made Jake so incredibly cynical and hard.

"Did you find a replacement for me today?" he asked in an obvious attempt to change the subject.

"No, but I've asked around and told people I'm looking. I'm running a small ad in the local paper next week." She stood. "I should go inside."

At once he came to his feet, catching her around the waist lightly. "What about Saturday night? Your sister could keep Katy and the doctor told you Ben will be in the hospital at least another week. Go dancing with me."

Maggie was aware of his hands on her waist, his closeness, the faint scent of his aftershave. She had thought about going out with him Saturday night, knowing she shouldn't, yet part of her wanted to.

Was she being foolishly afraid? She thought of her marriage to a man who couldn't settle and how his leaving had torn her to pieces. Jake was more of a wanderer than Bart was. If she didn't want to risk falling in love with Jake, she shouldn't go out with him. Yet every time a firm no rose to her lips, she found herself unable to utter the word. It had been incredibly long since she had gone out for even a few hours and she couldn't resist the fact that she found Jake exciting.

Exciting the way a wild tiger is exciting. "Jake, I shouldn't leave—"

"Katy will be fine. Your father is in good hands. You and I will have fun. So what's worrying you?"

"Don't act so innocent. You know why I'm hesitating."

"We're not going to fall in love," he said in a voice as warm and soft as melted butter. "I won't break your heart—you won't break mine."

"You sound sure of yourself," she said, annoyed by his confidence. His confidence made her reckless, and she slanted him a look, sliding her hand to the back of his neck. "You're so certain you won't fall in love with me," she said softly. "Maybe you should guard *your* heart." Emboldened by the startled flicker in his dark eyes, she stood on tiptoe and placed her lips softly on his.

In response, his arms tightened around her and he deepened the kiss until she was breathless and her pulse pounding. She broke away, wriggling out of his grasp. "All right, I'll go with you. Only make it a week from Saturday night. I'm still too worried about Dad to go dancing. And I'll guard my heart, Jake. But maybe you should guard your own."

But she wasn't guarding hers. She had just risked another searing kiss that left her breathless, wanting more.

She turned and hurried across the lawn to the house, moving with certainty through the darkened kitchen, knowing every inch of the house she had grown up in.

Later in bed, unable to sleep, she stared into the darkness and wondered who had hurt him so badly.

On Saturday afternoon a week later, Jake was driving a nail into place, rebuilding the rail fence around the yard when he felt as if he was being watched. He glanced around to see Katy nearby. She was sitting on a big red ball, watching him solemnly, and he noticed again what a little miniature she was of her mother with her thickly lashed, big blue eyes and her silky blond hair that hung halfway to her waist.

"Hi," he said.

"Hi, Mr. Reiner," she answered. Several times during the week he had found her nearby, watching him. The first few times, he didn't speak, but went on with what he was doing.

Thursday he had told her hello, and she had mumbled an answer. Last night there had been a sentence or two.

"When will you be through?" she asked.

"I'm about finished. Then I'll start building a new corral. I'll have to build a fence in a big circle so the horses won't get out."

"Are you going to build me a new swing then?"

It was the longest she had ever talked to him, and Jake turned to look at her. He nodded. "Sure thing.

But we have to find a tree to hang the swing in. Will you help me find a tree?''

''Yes,'' she said, getting up off the ball and grabbing it up to toss it into the air. ''We can find a tree now,'' she said, catching the ball in both arms and looking around. ''I can't go where Mommy can't see me. I have to stay in this part of the yard.''

''What's Mommy doing?''

''She's trying to decide what to wear tonight. Are you and Mommy going to have a date?''

''Yes, as a matter of fact we are. Is that okay with you?''

She tilted her head to study him. ''I guess.''

''Tell you what. Tomorrow afternoon we'll get your momma and all three of us will look around for a good tree for your new swing. We need a tall tree with a big strong limb. Want to do that?''

''Yes, sir,'' she said and turned to run for the house.

He watched her golden hair flying and thought she was cute. Maggie stepped outside, called to her and then looked at Jake. He waved and she waved in return. Mother and daughter disappeared inside the house and he knew Maggie was taking Katy into town soon. He finished the fence and went to get lumber to start rebuilding the corral. He knew he wouldn't see Maggie again until late afternoon.

He couldn't stop thinking about Maggie's final acceptance of their date. She had caught him off guard, surprising him with her answer, surprising him more when she pulled his head down to kiss him. Every time he remembered her kiss, his pulse speeded. From the first few minutes he met her, she had surprised him repeatedly. He wasn't sleeping well at night because he lay awake thinking about her, or he slept, dreaming of her. And he couldn't wait for their date tonight. Maggie in his arms dancing, Maggie to himself all evening. What was she feeling, he wondered. Was she as eager about tonight as he was? Were they both courting disaster as she had warned? He didn't think so. He had always walked away and he was certain she guarded her heart constantly.

With the sun hot and high, it was six o'clock when he put away his tools and quit working on the corral. He headed for the house. He still slept in the hammock, but he had to go inside to clean up. Maggie had given him a bedroom down the hall from hers.

As the screen slapped shut behind him and he stepped into the cool kitchen, his pulse jumped. Maggie stood at the sink with a glass of water in her hand. She looked beautiful and incredibly sexy in tight jeans, boots, a crisp, sleeveless blue cotton shirt. Her hair was drawn and tied with a ribbon behind her head. Fancy silver earrings dangled from her ears and a silver bracelet circled her narrow wrist.

"Wow, lady, you look great," he said quietly.

"Thank you." He could see a faint blush creeping over her beautiful face. "I'm ready to go, but I know you need to clean and change. I'll wait in the family room."

"I'll hurry," he said, wanting every minute possible with her this evening. "Don't go without me."

She smiled and he wished he knew whether her pulse was skittering as much as his was. He would know soon enough.

Five

As she waited, Maggie reminded herself again that she would take the evening the same way Jake would—it was to be a fun time they could forget and walk away from tomorrow. A night of fun memories, but nothing serious. And then Jake walked into the room and all logic went up in smoke while her heart thudded, and she knew she was committing a huge folly.

Wearing a crisp white Western shirt, jeans, boots, and a hand-tooled, leather belt with a silver buckle, Jake looked handsome and sexy. His tight jeans hugged trim hips and his broad shoulders filled out the spotless shirt.

''I'm ready,'' he said, walking toward her.

''We shouldn't be doing this,'' she said, looking up at him. He stood close enough for her to catch the spicy scent of his aftershave, see his smooth, clean-shaven jaw. His thickly lashed, dark eyes devoured her, making her drumming pulse accelerate even more.

"But we're going to," he said, taking her arm. "Remember, you're the one who warned me to look after myself. Getting scared now?"

"Let's go before I change my mind."

He held her arm as they went to her pickup. He motioned toward his bike. "Would you rather?"

"No, I'm committing one folly now. I don't want to compound it and commit another."

"Someday, Maggie," he said, holding the door handle, but blocking her way while he touched her cheek with his warm fingers. "Someday I'll get you to let go that reserve. I've seen glimpses of what it's like when you let it slip. One day, it'll go completely."

"Sure, Jake," she answered lightly, too aware of him. Smiling, she held out the keys. "You drive."

He helped her into the pickup and slid behind the wheel. They rode in silence for a time while she looked at her land, the burned and blackened fields, other fields that were turning yellow and drying up from lack of rain.

"You're making progress with the new corral." She finally said, breaking the silence. "Dad will be surprised and pleased."

"I'm trying to get it done before you bring him home."

"It'll be different when he comes back." She sighed. "I need to get my bed-and-breakfast going sooner."

"Hire some help and he can run the place without having to do much physical work."

"I don't want him to worry about it at all," she said, and Jake suddenly felt that he would stay far longer at the Langford place than he had anticipated.

He drove them to a local honky-tonk. As they walked through the rough knotty-pine interior with its dim lighting and raucous noise, people constantly greeted Maggie. The guys looked at her in a manner that made Jake place his arm around her shoulders. Looking around, he saw small tables circling a dance floor with an empty stage at the far end, and booths lining the wall.

"Do you know everyone in the county?" Jake asked after they had been seated with menus placed in front of them.

"I told you. I've lived here all my life. I probably do know everyone around here. I notice you're getting to know quite a few of them yourself. Watch out, Jake, or you'll take root like those big trees in our yard."

"Trying to scare me, Maggie?"

She laughed. "I wonder what scares you. I suspect there's very little."

"Oh, I can get scared," he said. He pulled a menu in front of him. "We'll see if Oklahoma ribs are as good as Texas ribs," Jake said, talking about different dishes and changing the subject.

She wondered what did scare him. Settling down? The thought of marriage? Since he lived on his bike, she suspected commitment of any kind scared him, but she wondered why. What lay beneath his fear of commitment and his declaration that to love is to get hurt? Was it because of the long ago fire that killed his family? She had an idea she would never know.

His dark eyes were inscrutable and he kept a wall around himself.

They were halfway through with heaping plates of barbecued ribs when Jake set down his soda. "A lot of guys here have noticed you, but there's one who's getting downright annoying. He's at the corner table."

She glanced around and looked into the pale, angry gaze of her neighbor, Weldon Higgens. Acknowledging him with a nod, she turned back to Jake and shrugged. "It's our neighbor to the east. We're not friends."

"Well, he's giving you a lot of attention."

"Yes," she said, "and I have no interest in him. Usually he keeps to himself. We had a fence down once and before Dad or any of the hands realized it, two steers wandered onto his land. Weldon killed the steers and told Dad to keep his cattle on his own ranch. No one else around here is like that."

"Want me to tell him to keep his attention to himself."

"No! Ignore him. I certainly can."

"If you can, I can," Jake said, giving her a lopsided smile. "The rest of the attention you're getting seems the normal, garden-variety notice of a good-looking woman, except I'm beginning to think I should have taken you to the next county where every male present doesn't know you. When the dancing starts, I suspect I'm going to have to share you."

She laughed. "There are all sorts of pretty ladies here who will be happy to dance with you."

"I've only seen one."

She smiled, enjoying his compliments and flirting.

"Besides, the looks you're giving other guys will drive them all away."

"I hope so. I don't want to watch you dance off in some other guy's arms. That wasn't the point of this evening."

"What was the point of this evening?" she asked, curious about his answer.

"To be able to hold you close while we dance." He leaned across the table to place his hand on her cheek again. "I want some slow-dancing where we can get up close and personal and I can feel your heartbeat and know that I'm causing your racing pulse."

"There are moments you have a real way with words," she said breathlessly, knowing he had caused another jump in her pulse. "I can't hide what you do to me, and from the very first, that's what's scared me."

Music started, and she remembered the crowd and pulled back, so his hand slid from her face. His eyes were burning with desire. "Rumors will fly all over the county about us and how you're living up at the house with me while Dad is in the hospital."

"I think it's common knowledge that I'm sleeping in the hammock out in the yard," he said with a big grin.

"After tonight no one will believe that."

"Maggie, if people are your friends, they'll want the best for you. The others don't matter."

"I suppose you're right."

"Let's do some boot-scootin'," he said abruptly and stood, taking her hand.

Relieved to break the tension, she went with him to the dance floor.

Musicians had filled the stage and for the next hour, Maggie two-stepped her way around the dance floor while Jake flirted and made her laugh. Between dances he kept his arm around her possessively so no one else would ask her to dance, which suited her fine. As she swept around the room with him, she realized she was having a wonderful time. It was good to dance and it was fun to flirt with him. It was also intoxicating to look into his soulful eyes and see the burning desire in them.

When the song they were dancing to ended, she excused herself to go to the ladies' room. When she returned, her heart missed a beat when she spotted Jake talking to Weldon who stood glowering at Jake with clenched fists.

Jake sauntered away, taking her arm and leading her back onto the dance floor.

"Did you threaten him?"

"I just talked to him a little."

"Jake, he's a neighbor. We have to live next door to him."

"He can stop staring at you like a stalker," he said gruffly. "The next time I see the sheriff, I'm going to tell him."

"Tell him what? Weldon is just staring at me. I told you that he asked me out some when I got divorced. To tell the truth, he gives me the creeps and I didn't want to go out with him so I think he resents that. But that's all."

"Maybe, but he doesn't have to glare at you all evening."

"Well, you don't have to worry about that because he's leaving." She pointed toward the entrance. "There he goes out the door. You ran him off."

"Forget it." Jake smiled at her. "Enjoy the music."

Annoyed she looked at him. "I'm not your responsibility. I can take care of myself."

"I'm sure your dad would have agreed with me."

"Don't bring Dad into this argument. And don't tell him about you and Weldon because I don't want him to get riled up. He's lost his temper with Weldon before and he doesn't need that hassle. Sometimes my Dad has a short fuse as several people around here know. Weldon killed those steers and now he wants to buy our place." Before she could utter another word, Jake spun her around and the argument was forgotten.

The next dance was a slow one and Jake pulled her close, wrapping his arms around her. She held him, aware of his warmth, of his thighs against hers.

They danced until midnight when the last slow dance played. Jake draped his arm across her shoulders as they went into the cool night to climb into the pickup. "Let's go home, Maggie, I want to kiss you good-night."

"I'm ready, Jake. Ready and willing," she said, flirting with him.

His arm tightened around her shoulders. "We're out of here."

Her pulse jumped and she twisted in the seat to study him. At a red light he laced his fingers in hers, and when the light changed, boldly placed her hand on his thigh before putting his hand back on the steering wheel.

Through the smooth denim, she could feel his warmth and feel the muscles in his thigh flex as he drove. It was a personal touch, an implication that she was willing to become more physically intimate with him and she debated whether to take her hand away or not. Yet she liked touching him and maybe she needed a little recklessness in her life.

When they arrived home, Jake opened the door of the pickup for her and lifted her out. For a second, he held her against him, finally letting her slide slowly down his body. Then he wrapped his arm around her and they walked across the yard until they were in the shadows of a tall oak.

"Maggie, I have never known a woman like you," he said, turning to face her.

"That's a stretch, Jake. I'm as ordinary as apple pie." She couldn't believe his words, yet they thrilled her. She knew for certain she hadn't ever met a man like him.

"This isn't ordinary and neither is what it does to me," he whispered. He tightened his arms around her, his gaze going to her mouth.

Her heart thudded, anticipation and excitement climbing. All evening long, she had watched him, wanting to touch him, marveling in the different facets of the man. She mentally reminded herself that she was just having fun as his mouth covered hers. The tip of his tongue began tracing her lips slowly. His tongue lightly stroked hers and ignited a roaring blaze within her.

Maggie clung to him, kissing him in return. He untied the ribbon around her hair and ran his fingers through the long strands. Dimly she was aware when he shifted and caressed her throat with one hand while keeping his other arm tightly around her. His hand slid down the blouse to her buttons.

"Jake—"

"Shh, let me touch you."

She knew he was touching her far more intimately than he realized, touching her heart. And yet, she wanted him to touch her and she wanted to touch him. She had a consuming hunger for this strong cowboy who had roared into her life and brought with him excitement and desire.

He pushed away the cotton blouse and his fingers slipped beneath the wisp of her black lace bra to caress her taut bud. She moaned, the sound lost in their kisses as sensations rocked her and urgency heightened.

Jake was so much more appealing than any other man she had ever known. He was a threat to her heart, but a temptation to her desire. Wanting more of him, knowing this night was unique, she tugged his shirt out of his jeans. She struggled with each button until Jake released her and yanked the half-buttoned shirt over his head and tossed it aside.

Her eyes had adjusted to the night and she could see his well-sculpted muscles. As he unbuckled his belt, she ran her hand across his smooth chest, stroking his flat nipple and then letting her fingers drift lower to his waist.

All thoughts ceased as he peeled away the straps of her lacy bra and cupped her breasts, stroking her nipples with his thumbs and sending shockwaves coursing through her. Momentarily lost, she grasped his waist and closed her eyes. Then he bent his dark head and took her nipple in his mouth, his tongue stroking her, hot and wet and driving away caution.

While he held and kissed her, Jake shook. He wanted her warmth and softness to thaw the cold winter of his dark past. He had half expected her to refuse him and keep herself shut away, yet giving was her nature. She moaned and trembled, her hands in his hair and caressing his chest, which heightened a need that was already raging inside him.

As they kissed, he unfastened and pushed away her jeans. They fell around her legs, caught on her boots. Sitting on a lawn chair, Jake pulled her down into his lap. While she kissed him hungrily and ran her hands over his chest, he yanked off her boots and jeans. He tugged off his own boots and dropped them.

"You're special, Maggie," he whispered.

Cradling her in his arms, he leaned over her, kissing her long and hard, his tongue going deep into her mouth and sliding over hers while his hand slid between her legs to caress her inner thigh.

Silent arguments rose inside her head to stop him now, yet she wanted him. She wanted to take a chance, to know him completely. When his fingers stroked her intimately, reason fled while she cried out and clung to him.

She heard a jangle of keys and then Jake flung his jeans over his shoulder and picked her up, carrying her up the steps and into the house.

"Jake, slow down," she whispered once inside the house before his mouth silenced her sentence. His arms were strong around her, his kisses escalating her need.

He took the stairs easily and walked into her bedroom. He set her on her feet, pulling her against him. Dropping his jeans, he wore only his narrow briefs and his body was lean and hard and marvelous. She ran her hands over his solid muscles, moving her hips against him, wanting him with a desperation she had never known before.

Caution was lost, vanished in desire. She didn't want to reason out how much she wanted or how much she was prepared to give.

Carrying her to the bed, he stood looking down at her and all she could think was how magnificently male he was. He peeled away her lacy black underwear and then he put one knee on the bed. As he leaned to trail kisses along her stomach, she laced her fingers in his hair. He stood and removed his briefs and her breath caught. She reached out to stroke him, sitting up to take him into her mouth and lick him.

He groaned, his fingers winding in her long hair and then he lifted her up to kiss her with such a hunger she thought she would melt.

"Jake—"

He laid her on the bed again, trailing kisses over her while his hand searched between her legs and then he stroked her till she was on the brink of oblivion.

Struggling to keep control over himself, he trailed kisses along her thighs while his hand continued to caress her. "I want to know every beautiful inch of you," he said in a husky voice.

"I can't reach you," she protested, sitting up to pull him to her. He hauled her into his embrace to kiss her and then he released her.

"Lie down, Maggie. I want to know you," he said, lowering her to the bed and rolling her over to trail his hands and mouth over her back and lower, down to her thighs. She raised her head and slanted him a look over her shoulder.

"Jake, you have to let me do the same—"

He was on his knees and looked into her eyes, his gaze blazing with his longing. "Next time, Maggie. You kiss me like this now and I'll explode. You don't know what you do to me."

His words shook her and she rolled over, flinging herself into his arms and kissing him, her need pouring into her kiss.

"Are you protected?" he whispered, and she shook her head. He stepped off the bed, retrieved his jeans and reached in his pocket to produce a small packet. Drinking in the sight of him, she stroked his thigh.

And then he was between her legs, wanting her, ready for her.

She wrapped her legs around him and he slowly filled her, hot and hard. While they moved together, her hands ran over his taut bottom and back that still was healing from the fire. In the far recesses of her mind, beyond sensation, beyond intimacy, she knew she was giving him far more than just her body.

Sweat rolled off Jake as he tried to slow and hold back, trying to make the special moment last, wanting to drive her to complete abandon. He wanted her as he had never wanted a woman before.

"Maggie," he ground out her name before kissing her, feeling her softness enveloping him. She returned his kisses while she was wild beneath him. All her cool reserve was gone as he had wanted. He didn't want their loving to end. She was fire and mystery and fulfillment. Thought fled while physical needs crashed in on him.

Maggie heard Jake say her name. She was lost in a dizzying spiral of ecstasy that wound tighter until a climax burst within her, and she felt his shuddering release.

With labored breathing, he trailed kisses over her temple. Taking her with him, he rolled over, his hand stroking her back while he held her close.

"I told you that you're special, but those words are inadequate," he whispered.

Shaken by his statement, she twisted to look up at him, and her fingers drifted along his jaw. Worry was already tugging at her, but wanting this moment to last, she pushed the nagging thoughts away.

She relished being in his arms. As she stroked his jaw, she turned his face to look into his eyes. "What is it, Jake, that makes you keep part of yourself locked away?"

He ran his fingers through her golden hair, letting silky strands spill slowly over her bare back and shoulders. He pulled her close against his chest where she couldn't see his face and was silent for so long that she wondered whether she had intruded into his private world too much.

"I told you, I lost my family in a fire." Jake's voice was ragged. He stared into the night, feeling Maggie's softness pressed against him, her arms wrapped around him. It was hard to answer her and it hurt badly, yet he knew if there ever was anyone to confide in, it would be Maggie.

"My parents drank, and my dad probably went to bed with a cigarette. The firemen said that the fire started with a burning mattress in my folks' bedroom." While memories assailed Jake, he was only dimly aware of Maggie's fingers that stroked him. Lost in recollections of that terrible night, he had a knot in his throat. "I was fourteen years old and wild and had slipped out of the house so I could go to the pool hall. When it closed, I wanted to just hang out with some of my friends. As I walked home, before I reached our block, I could see the flames. My entire family perished. My parents and my two younger brothers died that night.'' Jake clenched his fists. ''Maggie, I wasn't there to save them. They died because I wasn't there for them.'' The tormenting guilt he had carried all the years since swamped him momentarily, and he was quiet, gritting his teeth while pain stabbed his chest. ''I should have been there.''

She pulled away to look at him. ''Jake, you can't feel guilty about not being home! You might have died with them in the fire if you had been there.''

''I wished I had,'' he said bitterly, closing his eyes. ''I've never talked about this to anyone before,'' he admitted, knowing instinctively that there would be enough sympathy, warmth and understanding in her to trust her with his deepest secrets.

Hurting, he squeezed his eyes closed while she stroked his cheek. ''Jake, you couldn't help what happened.''

''I should have been there for my brothers,'' he argued, remembering the bedroom the two younger brothers shared. ''I could have gotten them out and should have. Damnation, how did we get into this,'' he snapped, annoyed that his dark past had intruded on a night that had been one of the best of his life.

As he rolled over on his back, she raised up on an elbow to look down at him, long strands of her golden hair spilling across his chest.

''We got into it because I asked you to share part

of yourself with me." Maggie stroked his shoulder. "Where did you live after the fire?"

"Foster homes because I was underage, but I ran away a lot. Then I was placed on a boys' ranch and that was my salvation. By the time I was eighteen, I got into rodeos and started winning money. I tried never to look back."

He turned to face her, his eyes pools of dark brown that were unfathomable. "If you love someone and they get hurt, you get hurt. I learned that the hard way."

"Oh, Jake!" she hugged him, placing her head on his chest and hurting for him. "Don't blame yourself. Your family wouldn't want you to and they wouldn't want you to go through life without love because of that terrible night."

He didn't answer and Maggie lay still, listening to his steady heartbeat. This strong, wild man was so tough and so guarded, yet at the same time, he had been kind to her father, so gentle with Katy and the horses, kind to her the night of the fire.

"Jake, love goes beyond physical intimacy." She sat up, trailing her fingers over his jaw, down over his throat, marveling at his strong body. "Why do you like rodeos and all the risks and roughness?"

"It's exciting and when I started, it was the most money I'd ever seen and it gave me a bigger sense of freedom."

"Have you ever been hurt when you've ridden?"

"Yes, but you mend," he said, turning to caress her, his gaze going over her. He swung her down on the bed and leaned over her. "Ahh, Maggie, I want you again more than before."

"I didn't know this was possible."

"Our loving?" he asked, kissing her throat. "'Course it's possible."

"No, the magic between us. You."

His chest expanded with his indrawn breath. "Damn, Maggie, I want you," he whispered and took her words with his mouth.

She wanted tonight to be special for him, yet at the same time, she knew that with every caress, she was heading toward disaster.

He moved over her, trailing kisses over her throat and down to her breasts. He was hard and ready again for her and she wanted him desperately because she suspected this would be the only night of love she would have with him.

This time when they made love, he pulled her on top of him, stroking her breasts while she moved with him until they crashed into exhaustion.

She lay sprawled over him, her golden hair fanned out over both of them. While he combed his fingers through her hair, her pulse slowed to normal.

"Come watch me ride in the Labor Day rodeo in Oklahoma City."

Maggie raised her head to look at him. "All right."

"Ask your Dad and Katy to come with us."

"They both love rodeos so I'm sure they'll want to go."

Jake rolled over so they lay on their sides. "Ah, darlin', I want to stay in this bed all day tomorrow."

"You can't," she said quietly. "When the sun comes up, the witching hour is over. Reality and responsibility return," she said, knowing what lay ahead and refusing to think about it for a few more hours.

"Yeah, well, for a while, you're mine. I want you all for me," he said, sliding off the bed to stand and scoop her into his arms. "We'll shower and come back to bed. All right?"

"Sure thing, cowboy," she drawled, knowing they couldn't shower together without making love again.

It was hours later when he slept with Maggie held tightly in his arms. Exhaustion made her limp, but she was wide-awake, thinking about the night and how foolishly she had rushed into his loving arms and given him everything. He was another man who couldn't settle, the wrong man for her. Yet in so many ways it had seemed right and wonderful. And so much more than anyone else she had ever known. She was in love with him. Jake had stepped in to help where he was needed. He was both strong and gentle. The knowledge that she was the first person in his life to whom he had confided his guilt about his family filled her with a mixture of emotions.

She ran her fingers over his shoulder, feeling his collarbone, sliding her hand down over bulging biceps. She lifted thick, dark strands of his hair off his face. He was a marvel in her life in so many ways, but she knew the day would come when he would say goodbye and leave.

In the morning, they made love again and then after staying in his arms for an hour, she slipped out of bed and grabbed a towel to wrap around herself.

"Don't go," he said. His hands rested behind his head and the sheet covered him below his navel. Each time she looked at his body or into his intense gaze, he took her breath away. Now it was daylight and she could see clearly the bulge of his taut muscles, his smooth tanned skin, and his lean frame.

"I have to go now. I told Patsy I would pick Katy up at church so I'm supposed to meet them there. You can come to church with me."

"Nope. I'll stay here. You could meet them after church and give us one more hour."

She leaned over him. "Forget that. You've worn me to a frazzle as it is."

He swung her down in the bed to kiss her long and hard, until she wriggled against his chest and he raised his head. Both of them were breathless, and desire burned in the depths of his eyes.

"I still want you more every hour," he said gruffly.

Her heart thudded because she wanted him and his words thrilled her. "Don't say I didn't warn you," she said, giving him a saucy answer and stepping out of bed quickly, walking away nude and knowing he was watching.

"Damn, woman," he said behind her and she slanted him a mischievous look, then rushed into the bathroom and quickly closed the door when he jumped out of bed and started toward her. She turned on the shower and ignored his call and the light rap on the door. He finally gave up and she showered and washed her hair. Last night was over, and now it was just a memory.

It would hurt when he left, but she refused to let her feelings for him grow.

She dried and dressed in a sleeveless blue dress, slipping into high-heeled blue pumps. With deft twists, she looped and pinned her hair on top of her head.

When she went downstairs, he was in jeans and had breakfast cooked. He turned to look at her, his gaze sweeping over her and she was conscious this was the first time he had seen her in a dress.

Six

"**W**ow, you look better than breakfast," he said, crossing the kitchen to wrap his arms around her and kiss her.

"You look yummy yourself," she said, kissing him and then moving away. "I have to get to town on time, Jake."

He studied her intently, and her heart drummed while she wondered what he was thinking. He merely nodded and turned to dish up bacon and eggs. He had poured orange juice and a glass of milk for himself.

"Want milk?"

"No, thanks." As she ate, she was too aware of him. He constantly touched her, eating little of his breakfast while he flirted with her.

After breakfast, they cleaned the kitchen and in minutes she headed for the door. He opened it for her and then when they went down the porch steps, he draped his arm across her shoulders and raised his face. "East wind—probably rain."

"We're approaching the record for number of days without rain. I hope you're right."

"But you don't think I am," he said, smiling at her. His arm tightened and he stopped her. "You're in plenty of time to get to church. Before Katy and your father are here, come for a ride on my bike with me. We'll just ride up to the main road and back."

"I'm in a dress," she protested.

"So who's to see?"

She stared at him, annoyed, tempted, and finally yielding. "All right, but you better get me back safely."

He framed her face with his hands. "I will always get you back safely."

"Don't promise what you can't deliver," she said, looking into his dark eyes.

"You are irresistible," he whispered, lowering his gaze to her mouth and kissing her.

Instantly, she pressed against him, a moan catching in her throat while her hips moved against him and she trembled. Her intense response set him on fire and he had to fight with himself to avoid picking her up and carrying her back to the house and making love to her. Instead he held her and kissed her and was stunned that each kiss just made him want more of her.

She finally pushed against him and when her eyes opened and met his gaze, his heart thudded. Desire was blatant in their blue depths. Her mouth was red from his kisses, and he wanted her with an ache that surprised him.

The Silhouette Reader Service™ — Here's how it works:

If offer card is missing write to: Silhouette Reader Service, 3010 Walden Ave., P.O. Box 1867, Buffalo NY 14240-1867

NO POSTAGE
NECESSARY
IF MAILED
IN THE
UNITED STATES

BUSINESS REPLY MAIL
FIRST-CLASS MAIL   PERMIT NO. 717-003   BUFFALO, NY

POSTAGE WILL BE PAID BY ADDRESSEE

SILHOUETTE READER SERVICE
3010 WALDEN AVE
PO BOX 1867
BUFFALO NY 14240-9952

Wordlessly he took her hand and led her to his bike. He threw his leg across the seat and sat down, helping her on behind him. She hiked her skirt up and his temperature escalated. He ran his hand along her tanned, smooth leg. "Beautiful."

"C'mon, cowboy, take me for a ride," she whispered in his ear.

He twisted to look at her and saw that mischievous, taunting smile that made him want to throw her down on the ground and kiss every inch of her until she was begging for him. "You know the ride I'd like to take you on."

"Start your engine."

"If you don't think my engine hasn't been revving since you came down to breakfast—"

She laughed. "Let's go, Jake, or I'm going to leave in my pickup."

The roar of the Harley broke the Sunday morning quiet. Jake eased to the road and drove slowly and carefully. He didn't want to frighten her and he liked having her clinging to him while they rode. How he wished he could turn onto the highway and just keep driving with her on through the day until the night.

When they returned, he slowed beside her pickup and she climbed off quickly. "That was an adventure."

"An adventure would be to get on the highway and see where it takes us."

"In the meantime, I'm off to church and I'll bring Katy back with me later," Maggie said as she climbed into the pickup and lowered the window.

He leaned forward, slipped his hand behind her neck and pulled her to him to kiss her one more time. When he released her, she gazed at him solemnly.

"Bye, Jake," she said, and put the pickup in gear. Jake stepped back and watched her drive away. He could still feel her soft lips parting for his kiss, her tongue going into his mouth, her body pressed against him. And all the memories of the night were still with him, yet he sensed that her goodbye had been final in spite of working here or seeing her every day.

She was the woman he would want to travel with him, but he wanted one who didn't need a wedding band, didn't want to settle, and liked the wind in her face on his bike.

Maggie was not that woman. She would want the wedding ring. She would want to stay forever in this part of the country. And he suspected she had little regard for his vagabond ways.

And then there was Katy. He didn't know anything about little girls. He would never want to disrupt Katy's life. Maggie had people who loved and depended on her.

Yet the night had been fabulous. Jake kicked a rock and turned to lock up the house and head for the truck to check on the animals.

Monday night Maggie glanced out the kitchen window and her pulse jumped as Jake parked the pickup and climbed out.

Tuffy ran across the yard and jumped the fence to greet Jake. Maggie watched as Jake hunkered down to pet Tuffy.

"So he won you over, too," Maggie said and walked back to the sink. After a few minutes, she watched Jake sit on the porch steps to pull off dusty boots. Tuffy came up beside him and Jake scratched his ears and she shook her head. "My dad, my dog, me. Next it will be Katy who will love you."

Jake had stripped off his shirt and held it and his boots in his hand when he entered the kitchen, while Tuffy stayed on the porch. Jake was covered with dust, a red bandanna around his head. In spite of his disheveled appearance, she wanted to walk into his arms.

"Where's Katy?" he asked.

"Watching television," Maggie said, jerking her head toward the family room. As he crossed the room toward Maggie, her pulse jumped. Aware how his gaze skimmed over her cutoffs and T-shirt, she inhaled swiftly.

"I'm too dirty to touch you, but I can't walk through this room and miss an opportunity for one quick kiss."

"Jake, if Katy sees us, I'll—" He silenced her with his mouth. Hot desire burst inside her and she returned his kiss, wanting him and knowing she couldn't walk back into his arms.

Shaken, she stepped away. "We need to stop," she whispered.

He studied her. "You don't know how great you look."

"Thanks," she said, feeling as if she were drowning in his compelling gaze.

"I'm going to shower."

She watched him leave the room, looking at his back that was healing fast from the fire. She returned to cooking dinner, her thoughts on Jake.

An hour later, Maggie passed a platter of golden fried chicken to him. He helped himself and set the platter down. "I have a surprise," he said, turning to Katy. "I made a swing for you."

Katy looked up and grinned, her blue eyes sparkling. "Can we hang it in a tree tonight?"

"Wait, Katy, say 'thank you,' before you start asking for more," Maggie said, smiling at her daughter.

"Thank you, Mr. Reiner," Katy said politely. "Can we put it up tonight?"

"Yes. And it would be easier if you called me Jake."

When she looked at her mother questioningly, Maggie nodded. "Jake is fine, Katy."

As soon as they finished eating, Katy ran outside while Jake helped Maggie clear the table. During the afternoon, Maggie had been to see her father. The doctor had said Ben could come home tomorrow because Maggie was there to care for him. Jake knew he wouldn't have her to himself after tonight.

With Katy present, Jake was circumspect, but he wanted to touch Maggie constantly. He stretched out his leg once during supper and brushed her leg lightly. She shot him a look and then they both were trapped, their gazes locked while tension snapped between them.

Now with Katy playing in the yard, he couldn't resist and caught Maggie around the waist, taking dishes out of her hands and kissing her before she could protest. And for a few minutes, she returned his kisses.

Then she pushed away and looked up at him. "Jake, Katy will be right back in here if we don't go outside."

"You're protesting, but your eyes and your pulse

are telling me something else," he drawled in a husky voice.

"Here she comes," Maggie said, and he saw Katy running toward the house, her long blond hair flying out behind her head.

"When are you coming outside?" Katy asked, bursting into the kitchen.

Maggie put dishes in the dishwasher and straightened up. "We'll be out in two minutes."

Satisfied, Katy left and Maggie gave Jake an "I told you so," look before continuing to clean. When they walked outside, Katy ran to join them with Tuffy tagging along behind her.

Katy pointed at an oak. "I know which tree—that one."

"Katy, we need a strong limb that sticks out far enough so that you can swing high. How about this?" he asked, jumping up and grabbing a limb on the oak with both hands.

Smiling, Katy nodded and Jake dropped to the ground. "I'll get the swing."

In a short time he had it ready and lifted Katy onto the seat. "Hang on tight, and I'll swing you."

Soon Maggie and Jake sat in lawn chairs and watched Katy swing. Tuffy sat beside Jake while Jake idly scratched the dog's ears.

"The dog loves you, my child likes you—you have a winning way."

"I hope so," Jake said. "After you get Katy to bed, will you come back out and sit with me?"

She was silent a moment before she nodded. "Yes. I have an intercom on the porch so I can hear if Katy calls me."

Jake's pulse jumped in anticipation. Memories of

Saturday night tantalized him and he wanted to be with her.

They talked until she stood and announced that it was bedtime. Katy smiled shyly at him. "Thanks, Jake, for the swing."

"That's fine, Katy," he said easily and watched mother and daughter walk hand in hand into the house. He sighed in contentment and then wondered if he was getting wrapped in invisible chains that would bind him forever. Could he ride away from here someday as carefree as he always had been?

He ran his fingers through his hair and wondered again why she was so special and what it was about her that made her different from every other woman he had known.

She came back, moving across the yard in the dark with the sureness of a cat. Moonlight spilled over her and his pulse jumped as he stood to meet her. Taking her wrist, he pulled her down in his lap, wrapping his arms around her.

"It's been a thousand years since this morning," he said, kissing her and reaching up with one hand to pull her hair free from her ponytail. In minutes he raised his head. "I'm moving upstairs tonight and giving up the hammock."

Maggie's heart drummed and she wanted another night in his arms. She stroked his muscled chest, tugging his shirt out of his jeans and letting her fingers trail across his bare skin.

"That's fine, Jake. Dad will be home tomorrow night, and if you were still outside, he would insist that you sleep upstairs. I got a lecture about your sleeping in the hammock."

"Serves you right," Jake said, kissing her again,

his hands going beneath her shirt until she pushed him away and scooted quickly off his lap. She pulled another chair close to sit beside him, aware he was watching her intently.

"Let's talk for a while."

"Sure. What about?"

She laughed. "Anything. You're going too fast."

"Okay, Maggie, what's the schedule tomorrow?" he asked, taking her hand.

"I think Dad will get to come home so I'll take Katy with me about eleven o'clock in the morning and if he's released, we'll bring him home."

"Need me?"

"Frankly I think you'll be needed more here at the ranch," she replied, thinking how much she did need him already. She wanted him to be with her, but she gave him the logical answer.

"That's fine," he said easily and stretched out his long legs. "Maggie, when the corral is finished, I want to bring Rogue up here so I can work with him in the evenings."

"You're crazy. Jake, I don't want to risk your getting hurt."

"You won't. I've worked with him daily, and he doesn't give me trouble."

"He doesn't?" she twisted around to look at him. "He doesn't—" Maggie broke off her sentence. "Why am I surprised? Jeb Stuart told me how good you are with horses. Dad's always been good with them, but he couldn't do anything with that one. I don't care if you bring him up here—we have the yard fenced so Katy can't get out and I watch her constantly if she's outside."

"Good thing you don't have a boy—he'd be going over that rail fence."

"Well, I'd be watching and I'd get him right back," she said. "By the way, the last time I was in town, I bought a cellular phone and a pager. I'll have the pager, but I want Dad to carry the phone with him in case he's out and needs help."

"Good idea," Jake said. He reached for her and trailed his fingers back and forth across her nape, stirring tingles in her that made it difficult to focus on conversation.

"Until Dad starts getting out, you can carry the phone with you."

Jake laughed softly. "I've spent a lifetime avoiding phones, clocks, and some of those things that are supposed to help life, but from my viewpoint, simply complicate it. Thanks, anyway. My health is okay."

"If you'd had a phone with you when you spotted the fire, you could have alerted everyone sooner," she replied.

"Point taken. If you want me to carry it, I'll put it in the truck. I'm not putting it in my pocket."

"Why not? Jeans too tight?" she teased.

"You don't like my tight jeans?"

"I love your tight jeans," she drawled and he groaned, stretching out his arm to wrap it around her shoulders. She wriggled away. "Down, fella."

"What do you expect me to do when you flirt like that?"

"Back to our talk. I would feel better if I knew you had the phone with you."

"Sure thing, Maggie," he answered, playing with strands of her hair, and she wondered how long she could resist him.

"I have six interviews set up later this week to hire some men to come work. I had ten replies to my ad." His hand stilled in her hair and then began to slowly comb through the strands again.

"That's good. This place is more than one healthy person can handle."

"I know. We've always had four or five men working for us until last year and things just happened until it got down to Dad only. But we'll go back to the way it was."

They were silent for a few minutes and then Jake asked, "Have your sisters ever traveled?"

"No one in the family has traveled much," she replied. "Tell me more about all the places you've been."

She listened while he talked, enjoying getting to know more about him and sitting close beside him with his hand constantly stroking her hair.

They talked for hours and yet it seemed minutes. Her curiosity never seemed satisfied when it came to him.

"Where were you headed when you stopped to tell me about the fire?" she asked when he had finished with a story.

"Nowhere in particular. I have the rodeo in Oklahoma City coming up so I would have stayed somewhere around there, but I didn't have a specific destination."

"You don't get lonely?"

"Sure, I do," he said, raising her hand and brushing her knuckles slowly with his lips.

She inhaled, knowing each touch increased the need for more of him.

"But when I stay in the same place very long, I get restless."

"Are you restless now?"

"What do you think?" he asked, his fingers tightening slightly on her wrist and he gave a gentle tug. "Come here."

Without thinking, she moved to his lap, and this time when his hands moved beneath her shirt, she didn't stop him for a long time. Finally she wriggled away and stood. He came to his feet at once and rested his hands on her waist.

"Come upstairs with me," Jake said, amazed how badly he wanted her.

"Jake, Saturday night was so very special, but I don't want to fall in love and suffer another big hurt when you leave. And I know you'll leave," she said quietly. "Won't you leave us?"

Pain stabbed him. As he gazed down into her wide blue eyes it was too dark to see her expression, but he could hear the anguish in her voice. And he could hear her determination. He had a feeling that Maggie would stand by what she said without wavering.

Combing her long, silken hair from her face, he let the soft strands slide through his fingers. "Maggie, I can't promise to stay forever."

"I'm not asking you to. I'm just telling you what I have to do."

"Damn, Maggie—not even tonight? This might be the last night before your father comes home."

"Jake, every time we're together, I'm more bound to you. First thing you know, I'll be hopelessly in love with you and suffering another heartbreak."

He framed her face with his hands while agony swamped him. "I don't ever want to hurt you."

"Then we have to say good-night now and each go our separate ways with our memories of a very special time." She stood on tiptoe to brush his cheek with a kiss. "Let me go, Jake. It's what I need."

She hurried toward the house, and he stood watching her, fighting everything in him that wanted to run and pick her up and kiss away her arguments.

"I didn't want to love ever again because it would hurt so badly to lose someone. Hell, I hurt now," he said to himself.

They hadn't known each other long enough for it to hurt this badly to see her walk away. Then again, he thought to himself, where Maggie was concerned, time didn't seem to exist.

He glanced down at Tuffy whose tail thumped against the ground. "What have I gotten myself into, buddy?"

He looked up at her windows. A light shone behind the shades. "I can walk away and I should," he said, as if trying to convince himself. Besides, Maggie had interviews to hire help, and then he wouldn't be needed here, Jake thought. He looked at Tuffy again. "You stay here. I'm going for a ride to see if I can find my way back to my life before I met Maggie."

He jammed his hand into his pocket to find his keys and went to get his bike. In a few minutes the quiet night was shattered with the explosive sound of the big engine roaring to life and then Jake swept away from the house, his dark hair flying out behind him.

Upstairs, Maggie stiffened when she heard the Harley. She slid out of bed and went to the window to raise the shade and watch him speed away. The pain that had been growing all day now threatened to overwhelm her. She could have been in his arms now, loving him, letting him love her.

Hot tears slipped down her cheeks unheeded and she wondered if he was gone forever. "He was going anyway," she whispered, reminding herself. However much it hurts now, it would have hurt worse with another night of loving binding my heart to his. Did he hurt? Did he care? This was the way he lived, she thought.

She straightened her shoulders, wiped her tears away and told herself the hurt would fade. She climbed back into bed and stared into the darkness. It was almost an hour later when she fell into a troubled sleep, only to be awakened by the sound of the Harley. *He's back.* She sighed deeply, feeling better, just knowing that he had returned. Had he just gone for a ride or had he started to leave and come back? Whatever the answer, it wouldn't matter later. The day would come when he would tear out of here and she would never see him again.

The next morning, Maggie learned her father would not be released until Wednesday. By Wednesday morning, Maggie had a dreadful time hanging on to the feeling that she was doing what was best as she and Katy ate breakfast with Jake. He looked incredibly appealing just in jeans and a T-shirt.

After breakfast, Jake stayed in the house to fix a leaky faucet and Katy sat on the floor to watch him work. For half an hour, Maggie worked on the ranch records, but then she put down her pen to go check on Katy. Pausing in the kitchen doorway, Maggie watched Katy play with Jake's leather gloves and ask him questions.

"Is she bothering you?" Maggie asked.

Jake slid out from under the sink and tousled Katy's hair. "No, she's handing me tools. She's a good helper."

"Fine," Maggie said, her gaze running over his long legs and tight jeans and broad chest. She met his gaze and turned abruptly.

Next he went outside to fix the latch on the fence, and Katy asked to go out and watch. Since Maggie had to be in the kitchen anyway where she could watch Katy, she gave her permission. She didn't expect to ask Jake to keep an eye on her child, even though she was certain he would.

Katy tagged after him and sat on the ground watching him. Once he stopped to swing her and he looked at the house and saw Maggie. He said something to Katy and Katy waved. Maggie waved in return and looked at Jake, wanting more than ever to fly into his strong arms.

Katy continued to follow him around until they both returned to the house.

Leaning one shoulder against the jamb, he stood in the doorway with Katy dancing behind him on the porch. "I'm going to work on the corral now. There are no horses in it, and Katy wants to come with me. I promise I won't take my eyes off of her."

Katy paused beside him. "Please, please."

Glancing at her watch, Maggie realized that with Jake watching Katy, she would have a chance to shower and dress to get ready to go get her dad. "All right. It'll be about half an hour and then I'll call you, Katy, to come get your bath."

"Okay."

They left, and Maggie watched them walk across

the yard with Tuffy trailing after them, Jake slowing his long-legged, ground-eating stride for Katy's sake. "Now we've all fallen under your spell, cowboy," Maggie said out loud, wondering how she was going to hang on to logic with Jake constantly around.

Half an hour later, Jake drove another nail into the corral gate. "Katy, you can hand me one of those hinges now. The black things there."

She ran to do as he asked and handed him a hinge. "Katy!"

As Maggie's call carried across the yard, Jake looked around, his breath catching at the sight of her in a red sundress.

"It's time to stop, Katy," he said, brushing dust off his jeans. "I'll go get Mommy's keys so I can bring the pickup around for her." He headed the same way Katy was going and as she trotted beside him, she slipped her hand into his.

Stunned, Jake looked down at her while his fingers closed around her tiny hand. She smiled up at him, and something inside Jake felt as if it shattered. He inhaled deeply, watching Katy walk with him with her hand in his. He slowed his steps so she would not have to rush. He had known Jeb's kids, but this was the first time he could remember a child placing her hand in his. The trust in Katy's eyes when she had smiled up at him had brought a knot to his throat. Maggie stood watching them and Jake got a grip on his emotions as they neared her. Katy turned loose of him and ran on inside the house.

"If you'll give me your keys, I'll get the pickup for you and bring it to the house."

"Thanks," she said, disappearing and returning to hand him the keys.

Assailed by her perfume, he took her hand. He leaned forward, trying to avoid getting her dusty. "One kiss, Maggie."

He covered her mouth and was lost in her fiery sweetness, aching with longing to have so much more of her. Finally she placed her hands against his chest and pushed.

"Katy will come back and if she sees us kissing, she'll have no end of questions and heaven knows when she will bring it up again."

"Would that be so bad?"

Her eyes were troubled, and she caught her lower lip in her teeth, making him want to kiss her again. "I don't think I want to answer a lot of questions about us. I better go." Turning away, she disappeared inside the house.

He left to get the pickup, but his thoughts jumped back to Katy and what it had been like to hold her tiny hand and see her trust.

As soon as he saw mother and daughter drive away, he left to make his daily rounds. With the drought, it was imperative that the cattle and horses get enough water. When he climbed into the truck, Tuffy jumped inside and sat in the passenger seat, giving him a pleading look.

"All right, you can ride along," Jake said, switching on the engine and driving away.

Along the western border of the ranch, he spotted a fence down and swore. It was the third time since he had started working at Maggie's place that he had found a fallen fence. Last time he'd had to chase down two steers.

There was a fence dividing this quarter of the ranch from the rest and Jake knew there hadn't been any cattle here that could have escaped. He climbed out of the truck and got tools from the back, then went to see what needed to be done while Tuffy trailed at his heels.

"Hellfire." Jake stared at two smashed fence posts and dry grass flattened by tire tracks. Someone had run off the road and smashed the posts. But then he saw another one smashed farther down the road. Vandals? Smashing a few fence posts didn't seem like it would be anyone's idea of fun.

Jake stared at the fence and then began to follow the flattened grass, backtracking across the pasture. Long ago, he had learned to hunt and track animals. As he drove slowly over the Alden land, he swore again. The vehicle had apparently crossed the ranch.

Seven

Jake needed a horse. Swearing, he climbed into the truck, waited for Tuffy to jump inside and then leaned out the open door while he drove slowly alongside the tracks where grass was broken and bent.

In minutes he went back to saddle one of the horses and headed out again on horseback, jamming the cell phone into his pocket.

It took another half hour before he found what he was looking for—a fence cut where the cattle were and six steers were missing. Grass was trampled where someone had loaded the steers into a truck.

Swiftly Jake yanked the cell phone out of his pocket and called the sheriff. As he waited for an answer, he watched the grazing cattle and realized no matter how many men Maggie hired, he wouldn't leave her until they caught whoever was trying to

cause her family trouble. Jake talked to the sheriff
and then he mended the fence, all the while stewing
with anger. Before today, he had replaced three
downed fences. Were they an accident or also an act
of vandalism? Cattle rustling was certainly no accident. It didn't hit him until he was riding back to the
house to meet the sheriff that the fire hadn't been an
accident, either.

Midafternoon while Jake worked on the corral, he
heard the pickup approaching. He put away his tools
and brushed himself off, going to meet Maggie as
she drove up to the back gate with her father and
Katy.

Dressed in jeans and a cotton Western shirt, Ben
was pale and thinner, but he swung his crutches out
of the pickup, stood and reached out to shake Ben's
hand. "Thanks for all you've done here."

"Glad to do it," Jake answered easily. "I'll get
everything from the pickup," he told Maggie as she
walked beside her father.

"Grandpa, I have a new swing!" Katy said, pointing to it.

"Good! I'll bet Jake built that for you."

"Yes, sir."

Jake got clothing and a small bag from the back
and trailed into the house after them to put things
away while Maggie got her father settled. When he'd
finished, Jake found Maggie alone in the kitchen.

"Maggie, I need to talk to you," Jake said. "Can
you step outside?"

Frowning, she looked past him toward the open
door. "As soon as I can, I will."

"I'll be at the corral," he said and left.

He hated that he had to tell her about the rustling.

He went back to work on the corral. In ten minutes he yanked off his T-shirt and rolled a bandanna to tie it around his forehead as sweat poured off his body. It was another twenty minutes before she joined him. She had changed to cutoffs and a T-shirt again, and as he watched her walk toward him, his pulse speeded.

"What is it, Jake?" she asked, moving close enough that he could smell her sweet scent of perfume. "Something wrong?"

"Yes. Your fence was torn down and six steers were taken last night."

"No!" Maggie whipped around to look at the house. "I can't let Dad know. He doesn't need any stress like that."

"Maybe he doesn't have to know right now. I spoke to the sheriff."

Turning, Maggie stared at Jake in surprise that he had taken charge, but she was grateful.

"Maggie, the fire was deliberately set. You've had fences down all over the place and I've had to chase down some steers. Now someone has smashed your fenceposts and driven across the ranch to take your steers. Someone is trying deliberately to cause you trouble."

"Why?" she asked, rubbing her earlobe as she pondered her own question.

"What about that cantankerous neighbor? It has to be someone who doesn't like your family or has a grudge."

"If it's a grudge, Todd Harvey is as good a suspect as anyone." Worries assailed her, foremost how to keep the bad news from getting back to her dad. "I don't know. Suppose it was coincidences?" she said, not wanting to cope with this new concern, yet knowing she was going to have to.

"Who is Todd Harvey?"

She shrugged. "He worked for us. He's from Rayburn—a small town west of here. Dad caught him stealing some tools from us and fired him. Since then he doesn't speak to any of us. He's been in and out of trouble, but he stays in town because he has a girlfriend there, so he's still in the area. Weldon doesn't like us, either, but it's difficult to imagine either one of them doing things like the fire and rustling. Todd doesn't seem like the type to have the energy for it, and Weldon would put too much at risk. He has a thriving ranch. True, he wants to expand and would like to buy part of our land. But what good would rustling six steers do him?"

"It seems likely to me that it's not a random act or a complete stranger," Jake said, resting a hand on her shoulder. "Someone is trying to cause you grief. Sheriff Alvarez said to let him know if you can think of anyone in the area who might have a grudge."

She rubbed her forehead again. "I don't know. Dad can be forceful, but other than the two I told you about, I can't think of anyone immediately. I don't want Dad to know this."

Jake glanced past her at the house and took her hand. "Come here." They walked around on the far side of the big flatbed truck where they weren't in full view of the house and he pulled her into his arms. "I wish I could take away your worries, Maggie," he said softly, and her heart felt squeezed in two. He spoke into her hair while he held her tightly. "I won't leave until we catch who did this."

Joy flared, and she let out a long breath. Jake

would be here a little longer. And it felt so incredibly right to stand in his arms. He was hot, damp from sweat, but she didn't care. His strong arms were a reassurance. She had a friend she could confide in and trust. "Thanks," she whispered.

"I left one other time in my life and when I came back, all those I loved were dead," he said flatly. "I won't run out again and leave someone."

Anguished, she tightened her arms around him and looked up at him. "Jake, don't continue to blame yourself for something you shouldn't have a shred of guilt about! Please, you were only a kid and you had nothing to do with what happened."

The coldness in his eyes frightened her as he shook his head. "I should have been there for them." He framed her face with his hands. "But I can promise that I won't leave you until this is over."

Tears stung her eyes for his hurt, for his staying and for the harsh knowledge that when it was over, he planned to go. He wiped her tears away with his thumbs.

"Don't cry, darlin'," he whispered, sounding as anguished as she felt. "We'll catch whoever it is."

"Jake, I'm not crying about that! I'm thinking about the pain you went through all alone…and I'm thinking about your leaving me," she admitted.

He wrapped her in his arms and crushed her against his heart and she held him tightly, feeling a shudder rack him. She wondered if anyone before had ever tried to comfort him over his loss. She knew he had never let anyone know his feelings about the loss.

When he turned her face up to his, he gazed into her eyes and the longing she saw made her tremble.

Standing on tiptoe, she closed her eyes and brushed her lips across his, taking his full lower lip in her teeth gently and running the tip of her tongue across it. He made a sound deep in his throat and then his mouth opened hers and he kissed her deeply.

In minutes their breathing was ragged and their hearts were pounding. She knew they didn't have any privacy and if she didn't get back to the house, she would have lots of questions. She leaned back. "Jake," she whispered, pushing him away.

She had seen him do all kinds of rough work and never get winded, but now he was gasping for air as if he had run for hours. Sweat beaded his forehead and the look in his brown eyes made her feel as if she were the most desirable woman on earth.

"All right, Maggie," he said hoarsely, stepping back and resting his hands on her shoulders while he appeared to be trying to pull himself together. "You don't know what you do to me, woman."

"It's only half of what you do to me," she said earnestly, thinking about her feelings for him. Her heart and soul were all tied up in a package with physical intimacy and she didn't think he realized it at all.

"Ah, Maggie. Why did fate throw us together?"

"I'm glad it happened," she whispered, and he hugged her again.

They were quiet while he held her and stroked her head for a few minutes and then he released her and moved away, keeping his hands on her shoulders.

"Back to the problem. I've had all morning to think about this. As soon as you hire some help, I can sleep in the daytime and patrol the grounds at night. I can go back to sleeping in the hammock, too.''

''No!'' Her hands rested on his waist and only half her attention was on their conversation. She was acutely aware of his warm flesh, his jeans that rode low on his hips. Too easily, she remembered him without the jeans. ''Don't do that. You sleep in a bed in the house. You could only see one part of the house from the hammock anyway. Besides, surely no one will try to get into the house with all of us there and with you upstairs. Tuffy will be on the porch.''

''Watchdog Tuffy. That dog sleeps as soundly as you do.''

She laughed and leaned back to look up at him. ''I'd rather have you in the house with us than patrolling the grounds at night. I'd feel safer.''

She had meant to step away and go back to the house, but the moment she looked into his eyes, she was trapped.

''I want you so damn badly, Maggie. And I want you more all the time,'' he said in a guttural voice. He bent down to kiss her again, and she was lost in a hunger that was undeniable.

Finally she pushed against him and he released her with his hands still resting on her waist. ''This time I really do have to go. I should check on Dad and Katy. If I think of anyone else who might have a grudge, I'll tell the sheriff, but I'm at a loss now.''

''Promise me you won't worry.''

''I won't while you're here,'' she said and walked away.

As Jake watched her go, he clenched his fists. He wanted her desperately with a need that overwhelmed him. If this was love, it was terrible. Or was the terrible part his emotions warring over whether to let go and love again? The idea terrified him. He remembered Katy slipping her hand into his and the awe it had given him. Mother and daughter. Family. Why did loving someone have to be so damned hard!

Swearing, he walked back to his work and watched Maggie disappear into the house. Images taunted him of her in bed with her silky hair falling over them, her body ivory and pink, soft and full of curves.

He swore again, working with fury, trying to chase all the memories and thoughts out of his mind, yet unable to stop remembering Maggie holding him so tightly and telling him she was crying because he was leaving her.

That afternoon he finished the corral and with expert handling, put Rogue in it. As soon as the gate closed, he watched the horse trot around the area with his ears cocked forward and nostrils flaring.

"It's a new place," Jake told him quietly, "but you'll get used to it and you won't have to stay penned up in here much. I'll be back after supper to see you." The horse stopped across the corral and looked at Jake and pawed the ground.

"See you later," Jake said and headed for the house.

During supper, Jake found himself caught up in the family conversation and enjoying their warmth. Maggie's blue eyes sparkled, and both Katy and Maggie had changed their clothes and looked fresh and cool. Ben was in jeans and a plaid Western shirt and his color looked better.

Ben set down his glass of water and said, "I saw

you brought that stallion up here this evening. Maggie says you want to work with him.''

''Yes, sir.''

''She said she warned you about him. I'd hate to see you get hurt after all you've done for us. That horse is pure trouble and no one can figure out why. I can't sell him, either.''

''I told Maggie, I'll take him, so don't keep searching for a new owner. I'm going to work with him in the evenings.''

''Don't say you weren't warned,'' Ben said. ''The corral looks good. I'll walk out there sometime soon and give it a close inspection. Thanks, Jake.''

''You're welcome.''

''I have a crew hired to start rebuilding tomorrow and Maggie has six interviews lined up, so we should get back in shape soon. It would help if we'd get a good rain.''

''I think we will in the next few days,'' Jake said, seeing Maggie frown and he knew she was thinking about someone trying to harm them.

After supper, Jake helped Maggie clean the kitchen while Ben and Katy went out to the backyard. Maggie tried to shoo him away.

''Go on outside and talk to Dad. Katy wants you to swing her and there's only a little left to do here.''

Placing his hands on either side of her on the counter, he hemmed her in. ''You know what I'd like to do here.''

''But you can't,'' she said, smiling up at him.

''Your smile could light the darkest place, darlin'.''

''Then I hope it's lighting the dark you carry in your heart, Jake.''

Before he could respond, the door burst open, Katy ran inside, completely oblivious of how close Jake had been standing to her mother. "Jake, will you please come swing me?"

"Sure, Katy, I'll be right out."

She left and he looked back at Maggie, a long solemn look filled with hot desire. Without a word he turned and left. Maggie closed her eyes and sagged against the counter. They were both tearing each other up every time they were together.

She went to work and looked out the window, watching Jake sweep Katy up into her swing and then step behind her to push her. In minutes he was laughing as he pushed Katy. She was laughing, too. "Damn you for charming all of us," Maggie whispered and then immediately felt contrite. "Sorry, Jake," she said aloud, even though he couldn't hear or know. It had been so good to have him here that she couldn't regret having known him.

The news that someone was trying to hurt them was tempered by Jake's strength and help and the knowledge that he was going to stay longer.

Outside, a breeze made the summer evening bearable while shadows lengthened across the mowed lawn. When Katy finally said she wanted to stop swinging, Jake went to sit in a lawn chair beside Ben who smiled at him. "Thanks for all you've done here."

"I was glad to be of help."

Ben reached into his pocket and pulled out a folded bit of paper and handed it to Jake. "Here's your first month's pay."

Jake took the check, opened it and frowned. "Sir,

this is way too much," he said, extending it to Ben. "I work hard, but not that hard. And I haven't been here a full month."

Ben smiled and shook his head, refusing to take the check. "Don't tear it up, son. When I was in a dilemma, you saved us, and I know how much I've let the place run down this year. You gave me peace of mind. How do you think you would have felt in my place with the ranch half burned and Maggie out here alone with a little girl? No, you take the pay. The doctor told me not to argue."

Jake smiled and tucked the check into his pocket, having no intention of cashing it. "Thanks."

"No, we owe you." Ben sighed. "I haven't hired people this year because I couldn't find men I could trust or who really wanted to work. With Maggie and Katy alone at the house, I have to be careful who I hire. It's getting harder to find help."

"If you'd get a horse trainer, you'd have some fine animals here. You have some of the best quarter horse stock I've seen. You could raise quarter horses, and it would be real profitable."

"That's what I started to do, but then I ran out of energy and that stallion was costly and too much trouble."

"He'll come around."

"If he doesn't kill you first," Ben said. Jake heard the screen slap shut behind them and knew Maggie was coming to join them. He stood and turned to watch her, enjoying the sway of her hips and her long bare legs moving gracefully.

"You interested in staying full time?" Ben asked. "Staying to raise those horses and train them?"

With a jolt, Jake looked down at Ben. "Thanks.

I'll be here for a while. Someday, I'll move on, but not soon,'' he replied swiftly, and wondered if Maggie heard him. ''Come sit down and watch the grass grow with us,'' he said as she got closer to them.

She laughed and sat beside Ben. Jake pulled a chair next to her. They talked until Maggie left to get Katy ready for bed and then as fireflies winked over the yard, Katy came running out in pink pajamas.

''Night, Grandpa!'' she said, climbing in his lap and giving him a kiss on the cheek. He hugged her.

''I'm glad to have my baby in my lap tonight and be home with you. I love you, darlin'.''

''I love you, too,'' she said and slipped off his lap to go to Jake, climbing in his lap without hesitation. ''Night, Jake,'' she said cheerfully and kissed his cheek.

He inhaled, hugging her lightly and smelling the clean soapy scent of her, and his heart opened like a flower to the sun. He had a knot in his throat and could barely speak. ''Night, Katy,'' he said.

As soon as he spoke, she was gone, racing barefoot across the lawn to her waiting mother. Jake glanced over his shoulder at Maggie who stood in the porch light. Their gazes met and he wanted her with a hunger that made him ache clear to his soul.

It was late by the time they had all gone inside. Jake changed and went down to work with the stallion. He put two powerful lights in the back of the truck that lit up the corral. Then he picked up a saddle and walked in. Since that first morning Jake had been with the horse every day, and now the stallion ambled slowly toward him.

''Tonight we'll progress a little more,'' Jake said

quietly, turning his back and walking away, knowing the curious horse would follow him. In minutes he had the stallion saddled, which he had done before, but he had never ridden him. He led the horse around the corral, talking to him, and then stopped to run his hands over him. Finally Jake took the reins and eased into the saddle and they moved into a walk. Jake knew better than to let down his guard. He patted the horse's neck. "Easy, easy," he said quietly.

He heard the screen door open and close and glanced into the darkness to see Maggie crossing the yard.

"Will it hurt if I come watch?" she asked.

"Nope. Not as long as you don't come into the corral or make any sudden moves."

She stood quietly, watching him as he rode, then finally dismounted and removed the saddle, bridle, and blanket. He was aware she still watched him and he had to fight the urge to fling down his armload and go to her. Instead he rubbed down the horse, fed and watered him and finally turned off the bright lights to go sit with Maggie and talk. Just having her close was good even if it was torment.

The next day the men arrived to rebuild, starting with the garage, and the place rang with the sound of hammers and power saws. Jake watched the ranch constantly for any new sign of trouble, but the weekend passed without incident. The week was the same until the weekend when they had three days of rain. By the following Wednesday, Jake noticed sprouts of green coming through the blackened earth. Nature was reclaiming its own. Soon, he knew, the blackened land would be gone from sight.

Time was stretching while he fitted more and more into his life on the ranch. The longer he was there, the tighter the tension grew between Maggie and him. They both were on a ragged edge and he knew it.

At night when he couldn't sleep, he paced his room and thought about his feelings for Maggie. The thought of life without her was like a terrible void. Always before, even when he had liked a woman, he had been able to leave without hurting, but the idea of telling Maggie goodbye tore at him. His life didn't seem right without her in it. Yet she would never leave this ranch, and what kind of vagabond life could he offer Maggie and Katy? He had always wanted to move on and he expected that urge to hit him again.

But was he in love with her? She was the best friend he had ever had, closer than Jeb whom he considered to be his closest friend. She was the most desirable woman he had ever known and every kiss made him hunger for more. "I love her," he finally admitted to himself as he stared out the window. The knowledge hurt because there could never be anything lasting to come out of it. She wouldn't leave her home and father. Ask her, he told himself. He wouldn't know until he asked her. He ran his hand through his hair and moved, feeling like a tiger in a cage. The walls were closing in on him and his body ached for her.

With the rain, they had a break in the hot weather. The temperature had dropped from the hundreds to the low nineties. On Saturday afternoon, Maggie stood in front of the mirror studying herself. They were going to Oklahoma City tonight to see Jake ride in a rodeo and afterward they would go eat with his friends, the Stuarts, who had come up from Texas. Maggie was as excited as if she had a date with him, but it wasn't a date. It was a family outing, and she wouldn't be alone with him once.

Her hair hung loose, cascading to her waist. She wore tight jeans, boots and a tan, sleeveless suede blouse that had a band of long fringe that ran from her right shoulder down to her left side at the waist. Filled with anticipation, she shook her hair away from her face and went to find the others. She had already dressed Katy in jeans and a blue blouse and knew Katy and Ben were downstairs.

She opened the door to her bedroom and stopped. Across the hall Jake stood facing her, leaning one hip against the wall.

"How long have you been standing out here?"

"It was worth the wait," he drawled, straightening and crossing the hall to her. He ran his finger along the fringe which crossed her breasts.

"You give a whole new meaning to fringe. I'll never see fringe again without thinking of you tonight. You look good enough to eat," he said softly and leaned down to kiss her. She returned his kiss briefly and then pushed him away.

"We need to go so we can see you do your stuff."

"You know what stuff I'd like to show you."

She smiled at him. "You look delicious yourself, Mr. Cowboy." And he did in a blue western shirt, tight jeans and brown handcrafted lizard boots. The leather belt circling his narrow waist was secured with a big silver belt buckle that proclaimed his winning saddle bronc riding the previous year. Downstairs he put on a black Stetson, and they all climbed into the pickup, Maggie riding in back beside Katy and letting Ben sit in front with Jake.

At the arena they had a box down front. In minutes Jake stood and waved to someone. Maggie turned to see a family of five approaching them. A tall, handsome, dark-haired man carried a little girl and waved in return.

Jake and Ben stood and Jake brushed Jeb's wife's cheek with a kiss, and Maggie faced a tall, slender, pretty redhead with lively green eyes.

Jake shook hands with Jeb before turning around. "Maggie, Ben, Katy, these are my good friends the Stuarts. This is Amanda and Jeb, and he's carrying Emily who is how old now? I think you just had a birthday."

The little girl held up three fingers.

"A big three-year-old girl," Jake said and then hugged the tallest boy. "This is Kevin," he said releasing him and smiling at him before turning to the other boy to give him a quick hug. "And this is four-year-old Brad, who is almost your age Katy."

He turned to Maggie. "This is Maggie Langford, her father Ben Alden and her daughter Katy."

When Jeb took her hand, he smiled. "So how did he turn out—like I told you when we talked on the phone?"

She blushed and smiled, glancing at Jake. "Yes."

"Ignore him, Maggie," Amanda said.

Jeb set Emily on her feet and in a minute all the children were together while the men clustered and talked and Maggie chatted with Amanda. In a short time, Maggie felt as if she had known Amanda far longer than only the evening.

The men left for their event, Ben going with them to talk to friends who were riding.

"I keep trying to talk Jeb out of riding, but he loves it," Amanda said. "The kids love it. They think it's great."

"I guess I've grown up watching rodeos and my dad ride. I used to barrel race, so it's always been part of my life."

She could see the curiosity in Amanda's eyes. "I've never seen Jake look at anyone the way he looks at you, and I never thought I'd see that happen."

Maggie blushed and looked away.

"I'm sorry if I intruded."

"Oh, no. It's just that there can't be much that ever comes of what we feel. He's got his life, and I have mine."

"That's what I thought one time, too," Amanda said, laughing. "Jake didn't approve of me when I first knew Jeb."

Startled, Maggie stared at Amanda. "I can't imagine that. Jake is so nice."

"He's protective of Jeb and he thought I'd hurt him. It doesn't matter any longer because Jake and I are friends now."

Maggie wondered again about Jake's past. So much of it was a dark shadow to her. She looked toward the chutes as the announcer's voice called the next event.

In the working part of the arena, while Ben stopped to talk to two old cronies, Jeb and Jake strolled ahead to look at their horses.

"I never thought I'd see the day," Jeb said.

Jake's head whipped around. "What?"

"You in love," Jeb said, with a flash of white teeth as he grinned at his friend.

Jake didn't answer. "Hell yes," he finally ground out.

Jeb sobered immediately. "So what's the problem?"

"What kind of life can I offer a woman?"

"A damn fine one if you want to."

"Wandering from pillar to post," Jake replied in a cynical tone.

"What's wrong with staying where you are now? Her dad seems to like you."

"He does. But you know I can't settle. Maggie has roots to the center of the earth. She's never even been out of Oklahoma."

"You might settle. Stranger things have happened," Jeb drawled. "Look at my marriage."

He turned to shake hands with a friend and in minutes the conversation was forgotten as Jake got ready to ride.

Jeb was the first one out of the chute, and Maggie watched, cheering and clapping his performance. A cowboy from New Mexico rode next and then Jake came flying out of the chute on a bucking roan and Maggie forgot everything else happening around her as she watched him stay with his horse. The roan was stiff-legged, leaping and twisting, Jake swinging his legs with one hand held high and she drew a breath, thinking how wild he could be, courting danger and risk, yet so tender and gentle. This wild cowboy took her breath and she knew he already had her heart.

When the buzzer sounded, the audience roared. Jake slowed and climbed into the saddle behind one of the cowboys who rode out to assist him. Then Jake dropped to the ground and left the arena.

When the tally was over, Jake beat Jeb by a point with Jake taking first place and Jeb second.

"He said Jake always beats him," Amanda stated with a smile. When the men returned, Amanda stood to brush Jeb's cheek with a kiss.

"I can't beat him," Jeb grumbled good-naturedly and sat down, pulling Emily into his lap while the other children were enthralled with a cowboy pouring out of a chute on a wild bull.

As soon as the rodeo was over, they all went to eat ice cream together. Afterward, the Stuarts told everyone farewell. Jake, Maggie, Ben and Katy watched them climb into a van and drive away.

"I can see why he's your best friend," Maggie said. "They're very nice."

"So are you," Jake said quietly in a low voice while Ben and Katy were climbing into the pickup.

Earlier, they had checked into a hotel in the city, Maggie and Katy sharing a room, Ben next to them and Jake down the hall. Now as they drove back to the hotel, Maggie rode in silence while Ben and Jake talked about riders and animals. She looked at the bright lights and traffic and knew the evening was coming to an end. She turned to watch Jake, seeing only part of his profile as he drove. His hat was pushed to the back of his head and his hair was thick and shiny black and she wanted to reach out and touch him. Katy's head lolled against Maggie's arm, and she saw her daughter was already fast asleep. Ben twisted around to look at Maggie.

"Honey, I'll sleep in the room with Katy. You

never get out, and Jake hasn't, either. You two go dancing or catch a late show.''

"Dad!" Maggie cried, embarrassed and chagrined. "Jake may not want to go dancing—"

"Oh, yes, Jake does," Jake interrupted quickly, grinning at Ben. "And I know just the place. Thanks, Ben. C'mon, Maggie, go with me."

She threw up her hands, yet in seconds her pulse was skittering at the thought of being alone with Jake, even for only the ride in the pickup. "I'm outnumbered here," she said good-naturedly and caught Jake's look in the rearview mirror that stole her breath.

Eight

At the hotel, Maggie got Katy tucked into bed. "Dad, I have the cell phone and I have your number and you have mine. If you need anything—"

"I'll call, honey. Go have a good time. Katy's asleep and we'll be fine. I'm not the sound sleeper you are, and Katy knows how to wake someone up when she wants something. Don't worry. Just go have fun for a little while."

"Thanks," Maggie said, smiling. Jake had carried Katy to bed and stood in the doorway waiting. As the door closed behind them, Maggie heard the lock turn. Jake draped his arm across her shoulders and walked to the pickup to open the door.

As he started the truck, she twisted slightly to look at him. "Did you and Dad plan this ahead of time?"

"Honestly, no. I'm as surprised as you, but I'm a hell of a lot happier about it. You almost refused."

She laughed. "I didn't think you should be pushed into taking me out."

"That really took some pushing. Come on, Maggie, let's have a good time." He hit the accelerator and they drove several miles to a large building with a well-lit asphalt lot filled with cars.

"The music is good here and there aren't many fights. 'Course if you'd go back to my hotel room—"

"Let's go dance," she said, climbing out of the pickup. He came around to walk close beside her, his arm around her waist.

"How do you know all these places?" she asked.

"That's one of the things that goes along with being single, riding in a lot of rodeos and riding my bike all over this part of the country."

"For a cowboy who doesn't drink beer, that's rather astounding. What's worse, I know you haven't gone alone to any of these places."

"You don't know any such thing," he replied with great innocence. But then his voice lowered, and his expression became solemn. "I swear I have never gone to one with a woman who sets me on fire with just one blue-eyed glance or keeps me from sleeping for a month or has me tied in knots all the time."

She stopped and looked up at him. "I do that to you?"

"Damn straight. That is the unvarnished truth. Or let me say it another way," he said, stepping close, pulling her into his embrace and settling his mouth on hers. Her heart thudded while dreams and lonely moments vanished and she hungrily devoured reality, kissing him in return. His demanding kiss left no doubt that she was desired. She could feel him shudder as she arched her hips against him. Holding him

with one arm around his narrow waist, she wound
her other hand in his thick hair. She kissed him long
and thoroughly and knew they had to stop or leave.
When someone whistled and a man cheered, she
pushed against Jake's chest. Two laughing couples
passed them and climbed into a pickup to race out
of the lot.

"Come on, darlin', before I do something out here
in public that will embarrass us," Jake said, taking
her hand to head inside.

For the next two hours, she was in his arms or
dancing fast with him, watching him and feeling excitement build to a fever pitch.

They danced until two and drove back to the hotel.
On their floor, they got off the elevator near Jake's
room, which was at the far end of the hall from Mag-
gie's and Ben's. Jake took out his key. "I have pop.
Come in and have a drink and talk to me for a while.
It's early."

"It's not going to make things between us easier."

"Maybe not, but come on. It'll make things a hell
of a lot better."

She entered his room that was almost identical to
hers with two large beds, a television, chairs, and
tables. He tossed the key down, switched off the
overhead light so the only light was one spilling from
the bathroom and pulled her into his arms.

"Maggie, give me a couple more hours of memories."

She couldn't protest. All the pent-up desire exploded in her. And she saw her hunger mirrored in
his dark eyes as his gaze went to her mouth and he
leaned down to kiss her. Her lips opened to taste and
take his strength one more time and the instant their

tongues touched, the fire in her blazed hotter. He turned so he leaned against the door and fitted her up against him. When she felt his manhood straining against his jeans, she knew he wanted her as much as she wanted him.

As Jake walked her back toward the closest bed, they shed their clothing. He ripped away the covers and they fell together on the bed. Maggie couldn't get enough of him, wanting him to let go and love and trust and not be afraid to sink some roots into living. Rediscovering his magnificent body, she slid her hands over him.

His hands and lips were everywhere as if he had never known a woman before and she trembled, aching for him, letting go completely.

With shaking hands, he yanked a packet from his jeans pocket. A few moments later he moved between her legs and entered her, taking her hard and fast and with a hunger that made her pulse roar. "I love you," she cried out, wanting him desperately.

"Ah, Maggie," he said, and then his mouth covered hers, ending words.

Warmth burst through her as she climaxed while he shuddered and moved spasmodically with his release. They held each other and finally slowed to lie quietly. He rolled over, keeping her close against him.

"Ah, darlin'. Stay with me for a couple of hours. Then I'll get you to your place."

"How can I resist you?" she said.

"You resist too damn easily," he said gruffly. "You don't know what I've been through night upon night."

"Oh, yes, I do know, Jake," she answered solemnly. "You're breaking my heart to pieces."

He cupped her face with his hand. "I never, ever meant to hurt you."

"I know. I didn't want to hurt you."

He pulled her close and they were silent for a long time.

"The next time," he said, breaking the silence, "will be for you, long, slow loving until you're crying out for me." Just his words in his deep, husky voice made her stir with desire and as he started kissing her throat, she shifted to turn his face up to kiss him.

True to his word, the loving was long and slow and it was half-past four when he walked her to her door, followed her inside for one last kiss and then went back to his room. As she closed the door behind him, she had a feeling she was really telling him goodbye this time.

The next week it rained for two days. Afterward, they had warm sunny days that brought out more green across the land. Jake walked out of the new barn that was now complete. It was the second week of September now, and Ben seemed to be regaining his strength daily. No more trouble had happened, so maybe it had been a case of strange coincidences.

It didn't matter because Jake knew he wasn't ready to move on yet. He glanced at the house before climbing into the pickup.

Since the night of the rodeo he was one big ache, wanting Maggie and thinking about her to the point of distraction when he worked. He was doing dumb things because his mind wandered, but he couldn't stop thinking about her. Without seeing his surroundings, he drove across the rolling land past trees that were beginning to show the first yellow leaves of fall.

He slowed and stopped beside an antiquated windmill that needed repairs and got out tools to go to work. Before he left, he intended to replace the windmill by plumbing the stock tank, but for now, he would fix the structure. He wondered if Ben had hung on to the windmill out of sentiment or simply out of neglect.

Midafternoon Jake wiped sweat from his brow and sat in the pickup to rest a minute. "I love her and I want her with me," he said to no one. Go ahead and ask her and let her make the decision, he argued with himself. Each time, he knew what her answer would be. She wouldn't leave her home.

Jake rolled possibilities around in his thoughts. Tomorrow he had to go into town for some wire and spark plugs for the truck. He would look at rings. He realized he might be the sole owner of the ring for a long time to come.

"Dammit!" he swore and hauled himself out of the truck to resume his work.

Out of a stand of scrub oaks Tuffy came bounding toward him, and Jake leaned down to scratch the dog's ears. "Where've you been, fella? You're a long way from home. If I could sit around at home and let her pet me, believe me, I wouldn't be out here."

Tuffy's tail thumped as he sat at Jake's feet. "I suppose you want a ride home. Well, you'll have to wait until I finish repairing this windmill."

It turned out to be the following week, mid-September, before Jake got into town. After running errands, he went to a jewelry store and found a ring he liked. He wondered what he would do with it when she refused to take it. In the quiet of the store, he stood staring at a two-carat solitaire and was lost in memories of Maggie in his arms, gazing up at him with her eyes filled with desire.

"That's a beautiful diamond," the clerk said.

"Yes, it is. I'd like to think about it," Jake replied gruffly, knowing it had never taken him this long in his life to buy anything. The clerk moved a discreet distance away and waited patiently.

Jake turned the stone, catching glints of dazzling light. Was he delaying because he was sure Maggie would refuse—or because he was uncertain of himself? As fast as he asked himself the question, he knew he was deeply in love. How had she gotten past all his defenses so easily?

He swore under his breath and caught the clerk's eye.

The man returned. "Yes, sir?"

"This is the ring I want and I have a string here that I put around her finger, so maybe you can tell the size from this."

"Yes, sir. That's a beautiful choice, and I'm sure she'll be thrilled with it."

Jake wasn't sure at all. While the clerk wrote up the ticket and put away the ring, Jake remembered sitting in the family room with Maggie late one night last week. After Katy and Ben had gone to bed, Jake and Maggie had watched a movie, although neither one had seen half the movie because they talked all the way through it. While they talked, he had pulled

a string from his pocket that he had put there earlier
and looped it around her finger, tying it.

"What are you doing?" she asked, laughing, her
dimple showing.

"Tying you to me," he said, looking into her eyes
and her laughter vanished.

He slipped the string off her finger and tucked it
away. He wondered whether he was off with his
hasty and poor measurement, but he thought he'd be
close enough.

"We'll have that ready a week from tomorrow,
sir," the clerk said when he returned.

Jake finished the transaction and finally left the
store, not feeling much better than he had when he
went in.

Tuesday night a week later, Maggie showered and
changed for bed. She had sat on the lawn until three
talking to Jake, and she was too aware he was just
down the hall, yards away yet light years from her.

Sleep was impossible because all she wanted was
to be in his arms. Each day she knew he was slipping
away more from her. If only he could let go of old
hurts. Every time she had that thought, she knew that
even if he did open his heart and love her, he
wouldn't settle down. The day would come when he
would have to move on and she and Katy could not
go with him.

Moving restlessly to the window, Maggie looked
down at the empty hammock and remembered that
first night Jake had been with them. Now they had a
new barn, garage and corral, and she was head-over-
heels in love with a vagabond cowboy.

She sank down on a rocker and put her arms on

the windowsill, resting her head in her hands while she finally let loose a watershed of tears that she'd locked away for a long time.

When she was through, she wiped her eyes and began rocking, wondering if the hurt would even stop in this lifetime. She didn't know how much time passed when a movement in the yard caught her eye. She stiffened as a dark shadow drifted toward the garage.

Someone was walking around the garage and she didn't think it was Jake. The new hands she had hired all lived in town and went home at night. Anger shook her that someone might be trying to cause them more trouble.

Furious and determined to catch whoever it was, she ran across the room, yanking on her cutoffs and pulling a T-shirt over her head. Jamming her feet into sneakers, she raced downstairs where she stopped at the hall closet to get her father's shotgun from a high shelf.

Dashing across the porch, she stepped over a sleeping Tuffy. As she hurried across the yard, she slowed to move with more care. All she could think about was someone starting another fire and she couldn't bear for her father to have to go through another big disaster.

Looking at the darkened garage, she slowed and listened. Crickets chirped and there were faint rustlings. Then metal clinked against metal.

Maggie crept forward cautiously, going around the side of the garage. Shocked, she stared at the dark silhouette of a man who was leaning under the hood of the pickup.

* * *

Restless, unable to sleep, Jake stood at the upstairs window. He paced the room and moved back to the window, looking out at the dark night when a movement of white caught his eye. He frowned when he recognized Maggie's long hair, pale in the night. Then he spotted the silhouette of a gun in her hand.

"Dammit!" He yanked on jeans and ran. He didn't know what or who she was after, but she had no business going out alone.

Terrified for her safety, he took the stairs two at a time and ran out the back door, wanting to shout her name, but afraid he might make a dangerous situation worse.

He caught sight of her ahead of him and then she disappeared around the corner of the garage. Stretching out his legs, he ran headlong after her.

Nine

Maggie raised the shotgun and pointed it at the man who was leaning under the hood of the pickup. "Move away from the truck with your hands in the air," she snapped. Her heart pounded with fury that someone was trying to do them more harm.

The man straightened, turning toward her. Then he lunged at her, hitting the shotgun and knocking her down. Sharp pain stabbed her side and arm.

Yelling, Maggie scrambled to her feet. While she tried to find the shotgun, she heard her assailant running away.

Approaching her rapidly, footsteps pounded behind her. Her heart thudded with fear that there might be two intruders until she recognized Jake's dark silhouette.

"Call the sheriff!" he yelled as he dashed past her, racing after the man.

She yanked up the shotgun and turned to hurry back to the house.

With shaking hands she dialed 911 on a cordless phone and told the dispatcher about the intruder. "Whoever comes, please ask them to keep the sirens off. My father is back from the hospital—"

"Maggie, this is Ida Holmes. They won't turn on sirens. Tell me what happened."

"Thanks, Ida," Maggie said and tried to relay everything as it had happened. While they talked, she walked outside, peering into the darkness, wondering how long it would take the sheriff to send someone out.

She was worried about Jake's safety, and she began to feel stings and aches from her fall.

It seemed like eternity until she saw flashing lights through the trees. The cars pulled up in front of the house and the sheriff got out and closed his door quietly.

"Where is he now?" Ty Alvarez asked her as three men climbed out of the other car.

"We were by the pickup and he knocked me down and ran," Maggie replied. "Jake took off after him," she said, pointing the direction she had last seen them. "I ran back here and called you."

"Stay here and keep the house locked up," the sheriff said and motioned to the men. With guns drawn, all four fanned out, and she was even more afraid for Jake's safety. She worried that Jake would mistake a lawman for the intruder. Or that they would mistake Jake for her assailant.

Except for the back door, the house was locked. She went inside and returned her father's shotgun to its place on a high shelf in the closet, far out of reach of Katy. Switching off the downstairs lights, she went to the backyard, sitting on a lawn chair in the darkness, mulling about what had happened and hoping they caught the man.

The intruder was tall. She knew that much, but nothing else. She didn't have time to see his face so she couldn't give the sheriff a good description.

Her hip hurt where she had fallen, and her ribs ached where he had tackled her. Her elbow stung, but she didn't care. She tugged her earlobe and worried, wishing the men would return, wanting to see Jake safely home. She glanced back at the house, thankful her father and Katy were sleeping through all this. Staring into the darkness, she tugged her ear nervously. Where were they?

When she saw figures moving out of the darkness, she had to curb the urge to run to them. The moment she spotted Jake's tall silhouette, her heart thudded with relief.

As she walked toward the police cars, she realized they had caught someone.

Curious and angry, she was relieved to see that Jake was all right.

Jake hurried over to her and slid his arm around her waist. His cheek was scraped, he had a cut on his shoulder and he was smudged with dirt. She inhaled, wanting to touch him.

"Are you all right?" Jake asked.

"Yes," she answered.

As one of the lawmen turned on his headlights, she glanced around, looking into the angry gaze of her neighbor.

"Weldon!"

Covered with cuts, welts and dirt, with a swollen

mouth and one eye swollen shut, Weldon Higgens stood glaring at her.

Besides his injuries, Weldon's T-shirt was ripped and bloodstained. She wondered if Jake had done all that to him. She blinked at the hate she could see in his expression. Stunned, she could only stare at him in amazement. "Why?" she whispered, but no one answered.

Lawmen hauled him away to put him into the back of a car while Sheriff Alvarez walked over to her. "Jake got Weldon to confess that he's the one who has been causing all the trouble around here."

"The fire?" she asked, horrified that it was deliberately set by someone they knew.

Ty Alvarez nodded grimly. "When Higgens gets out of jail—and I hope that's a long time from now—he'll have to move out of these parts. No one will want him around. That fire threatened all of us and could have cost lives."

"Why did he want to harm us?" Maggie repeated, surprised and mystified.

"I intend to find out all about it," the sheriff said, glancing in Weldon's direction. He turned back to Maggie. "I'll send someone out to get a statement from you, Maggie."

"Thanks for coming so quickly."

Suddenly he grinned. "Bet it didn't seem quick at the time."

"No, it didn't."

"You said he knocked you down. How badly are you hurt?"

"Nothing serious."

He nodded. "Thanks, Jake." Ty climbed into the other car and both cars turned, driving away.

The moment their taillights were going down the road, Maggie turned to Jake. "You're hurt."

"I'm all right. What about you?"

"My ribs hurt and my elbow and my hip."

"Let's have a look," he said, striding toward the house. "Where's the shotgun?"

"I put it on the top shelf in the hall closet."

He stopped and looked down at her, holding her shoulders. "Maggie, Uncle Sam trained me for combat. There should never be a next time, but if there is, will you come get me instead of running after the guy yourself?"

Astounded, she stared at him. But her surprise was quickly replaced by annoyance. "Jake, next time you may be in another state. I didn't think. I reacted. I wanted to stop whoever it was and keep them from doing something else that would hurt my dad."

"If I'm here," Jake said evenly, "will you come get me?"

"I'll try to remember that you asked," she said with a lift of her chin.

"Come on."

She fell into step beside him. "Why? Why would Weldon do those things to us?"

"He confessed to me. Your bed-and-breakfast."

Her mouth dropped open. "Why the bed-and-breakfast? I don't even have one yet. That's just plans in the future."

"He was afraid of people coming out here and ruining his privacy and ranch life and trespassing on his place. Also, I think he's angry you wouldn't go out with him."

"Oh, my word," she said, rubbing her forehead,

shivering and suddenly aware of the dark night and aware of her vulnerability when she went after him.

"Yeah. Come on. Let's look at your injuries." Jake put his hand across her shoulders and walked up the steps with her. At the top she turned to look at the new buildings and corral, and the dead, leafless trees across the lane.

"How could he hate enough to do something so terrible? Dad could have died in the barn if you hadn't been here to get him."

"When it comes to hate, no one can figure out the way some people's minds work. It's over, Maggie. Higgens is going to jail and then he'll be smart to leave this county."

Jake locked up and they went upstairs to his room. As soon as he switched the light and looked at her, he swore. "Damn him. I'd like to hit him again. Do you have any bandages?"

She studied her scraped and bloody elbow. "I'll be right back." She left and in minutes returned, holding antiseptic, gauze, bandages and tape. As soon as Jake shed his boots and shirt, she looked at a cut across his shoulder.

"You're hurt, too."

"Only a scratch. Let's go into the bathroom."

He led her into the high-ceilinged bathroom with its footed tub and lacy curtains. She washed her arm and then Jake dried it gently and sat on the edge of the tub, pulling her between his legs to bandage her scrapes. As he applied antiseptic, she inhaled swiftly. It stung and she bit her lip.

"Just be glad you aren't hurt worse," Jake said darkly. "It could have been a lot worse you know."

She looked down at him. "Are you trying to scare me?"

His dark eyes were fiery. "Do you know what a scare you gave me?"

Her heart skipped a beat. "Did I?" she asked, suddenly interested in how concerned he was over her welfare.

"Damn straight you did," he snapped, wrapping gauze around her arm. "Hold this, Maggie."

"How did you know I was outside?" she asked, placing her finger on the gauze until he could put tape on it.

"I saw you out my window."

"Couldn't sleep?"

"No, I couldn't sleep," he replied slowly.

"Well, neither could I. That's why I saw someone out in the yard." When he met her gaze again, she drew a sharp breath at the smoldering fires in his eyes. Their gazes locked and her heart drummed and finally he looked down at her arm. "That's finished. Let me look at your ribs."

"Jake—" she said, but he had already tugged up her T-shirt just below her breasts and, with the seeming clinical detachment of a doctor, was feeling her ribs.

"Ouch!"

"Sorry. Does it hurt to breathe?"

"No, but I don't want to cough."

"I don't think you have any broken ribs, but you've probably bruised them. Same with your hip."

She yanked down her T-shirt. "Thanks, Dr. Reiner."

Standing, he framed her face and looked at her

with an intensity that sobered her. "I mean it, Maggie. When I'm here, don't go chasing someone."

"I don't think it'll ever come up again. They've arrested Weldon."

"You're not giving me the reassurance I want."

"Jake," she said, becoming annoyed with him again. "The next time something happens—and I hope that's never—you could be ten states away."

"But if I'm here, Maggie—"

"All right. If you're here, I'll let you know."

"Lord, woman, I can't tell you what that did to me," he said, enveloping her in a gentle embrace and it was good to be in his arms. He was careful of her ribs, holding her lightly.

"The best thing for bruises like that is steamy water. Come on, I'll show you." He tugged off her shirt before she could protest.

"Jake, no—"

"Yes. You'll feel one hundred percent better. I've hurt my ribs enough to know." All the time he talked, he was twisting free buttons on her jeans, shedding his own and in seconds, she forgot her arguments as he stepped into the shower and pulled her in with him.

Hot water hit them and she looked up at him, slanting him a look. "What you do to me—" she whispered and stood on tiptoe to kiss him.

For the next hour she forgot her scrapes and aches as they loved and Jake was careful of her ribs, yet setting her on fire with his caresses and kisses.

Later, as she lay in his arms, she glanced at the clock. "It's after four in the morning!"

"There's still time before everyone stirs."

She slid out of bed. "No. I'm going to my room,"

she said, swinging her hair away from her face and gathering her clothes, getting dressed swiftly. She turned to find Jake with his head propped on his hand, watching her. Shedding a soft glow in the bedroom, a light still burned in the bathroom, and she blushed.

"Don't stare."

"You're beautiful, Maggie," he said hoarsely. "I wish you'd come back here."

"No. I have to go."

He was out of bed and past her, blocking her way at the door. "I want a kiss."

She stared at him and then wrapped her arms around his neck, standing on tiptoe and placing her mouth on his to kiss him with all the longing and passion she had. She wanted to melt him, to do to him half of what he did to her. Even more, she wanted to win his heart and love as he had won hers so easily.

Jake's arms tightened around her waist and his hand slid over her bottom, pulling her up hard against him while he kissed her in return. Her heart thudded and in minutes she pushed away because if she didn't, she would be back in bed with him.

"I'm going," she whispered and fled, hurrying barefoot down the hall to her room where she closed the door behind her without looking back.

In bed, she thought about the night, still stunned about their neighbor, but forgetting him as she thought about Jake and their lovemaking. How much longer would Jake stay with them?

"I love you," she whispered, feeling hot tears sting her eyes. She had fallen in love with a man who would never love in return. She hurt for herself and she hurt for him because he was shutting himself into a lonely life.

She rolled over and pounded the bed with her fist. "Jake!" she cried against the pillow, knowing all sound was muffled.

She slept fitfully to wake early. Worrying about breaking the news to her father about Weldon, she dressed and went downstairs to cook breakfast.

In the kitchen Jake had coffee brewing and orange juice poured. He stood by the stove, stirring a steaming pot. Her gaze ran over his jeans and T-shirt, his hair shaggy, black. She wanted to cross the room and walk into his arms. Instead, she reminded herself to keep a distance between them.

"Good morning. What're you cooking?" she asked as she crossed the room to look at the stove.

"Oatmeal for everyone. I hope everyone eats all this."

"They will. Thanks."

"Think the news will upset your dad?"

"I don't know."

"What will upset your dad?" Ben asked, entering the room and Maggie smiled at him as he carefully crossed the kitchen on his crutches.

"You talk about how soundly I sleep—last night you slept right through a lot of excitement," she said.

"Is that right? 'Morning, Jake. What're you cooking?"

"Oatmeal and it's ready. Sit down and I'll serve."

In minutes all three were seated and Ben lowered his glass of orange juice. "All right. What did I sleep through?"

"There was someone in the yard. Jake went after the intruder," Maggie said, skipping the fact that she had gone after him first and aware Jake was studying her. "I called Ty Alvarez and they caught him. It was Weldon, Dad."

As he dropped his spoon and swore, Maggie reached over to touch his hand. "Now don't get excited. The police have him and he'll be charged. Weldon Higgens isn't worth you getting your blood pressure up."

"Don't fuss over me, Maggie. I'm not going to injure myself swearing about Higgens. He set the fire?"

"He confessed everything to me when I had him pinned down," Jake answered. "He didn't want a bed-and-breakfast drawing a crowd out here and running down the value of his ranch."

"Sonofagun!" Ben snapped. "Weldon! I never did like him very much, but I didn't think he was downright evil."

Jake looked at Ben. "I also don't think Higgens was happy that Maggie wouldn't go out with him," Jake added.

Ben snorted derisively. "I didn't think he was so damn dumb, either. Now he'll be in jail instead of running that ranch he thinks so much about. Well, damn. Why didn't you wake me?" he asked Maggie.

"I didn't see the point. You're hearing about it now, and why get you up?"

"I can't believe I slept through the sheriff coming out here. What was Higgens up to last night anyway?"

"I don't know," Maggie said. "He was under the hood of the pickup—"

"I told Alvarez about that," Jake said, smoothly interrupting her. "He's coming out here to look at the pickup this morning. Until he does, we can't drive it. That may be part of their case."

"I forgot all about the pickup," Maggie said.

"I didn't," Jake replied. "I want to hang around here until the sheriff gets here. In the meantime, I need to ask you about moving some things from the shed to the barn," Jake said to Ben.

"After breakfast we'll go look."

They talked about Weldon and then the conversation changed until breakfast was over. Then he and Ben walked out toward the barn. As he did, Jake glanced over his shoulder and looked into Maggie's eyes. He paused for an instant, taking one last long look at her. She was in jeans and a sleeveless blue shirt with her hair braided. She looked as fresh and rested as if she had been undisturbed all night. All he was thinking about was Maggie in the pale light of the bedroom in the early hours of the morning when she was naked, in his arms and raising her mouth eagerly for his.

"See you," he said, unable to keep the huskiness out of his voice.

Hurrying, he caught up with Ben. "Ben, where do you keep your shotgun?" he asked, already knowing the answer.

"It's in the hall closet on the top shelf where Katy can't possibly get to it. She can't climb on a chair and reach up there. She's never in there, anyway, because there's nothing in the closet of hers." Ben glanced his way. "How'd you know I have a shotgun?"

"Maggie saw Weldon first and she got your gun and went after him. I happened to see her going across the yard and took off after her."

"Oh, hell. Maggie just acts. I'm sure she was trying to protect me from getting upset or getting into something that might hurt me. Dammit! I hate being feeble!"

"You're getting stronger every day," Jake said. "If anything ever happens again, I asked her to get me, but I was wondering if you could find another place for your gun."

"There's a high shelf in the closet in my bedroom. I'll put it there. Katy's never in my closet and she couldn't get up there, either. Just to be on the safe side, I guess I'll unload it."

"It'll be safer that way. Maybe now you won't have any more bad incidents."

"That bastard. What could he expect to gain?"

"He was trying to drive you folks out. Alvarez said Higgens is finished in these parts because when he does get out of jail, no one will welcome him around here."

"Thanks, Jake, for coming to the rescue again."

"On another subject," Jake said. "I'd like to ask Maggie out Saturday night."

"Go right ahead. I'm well enough to stay with Katy and if Maggie is worried about her, she can take Katy in to spend the night with her cousins. I'll be fine. Better yet, Patsy has been wanting me to come stay with them for a few days. I'll take Katy Saturday, and we'll stay at Patsy's house. Then Maggie won't have to worry about either one of us."

"Thanks, Ben," Jake said and wondered how long before he would have a chance to ask Maggie about Saturday.

"Jake, when Ty comes out to look at the pickup, I wish you'd get me."

"Sure," Jake said.

An hour later both men stood watching while Ty looked beneath the hood of the pickup. His deputy was underneath the front end. Jake wanted to join them, but knew he'd be in the way.

"He cut the brake lines," Ty said, straightening. "We've got another stiff charge to add to the ones he already has."

"With no brakes, we all could have been killed," Ben said in a cold, deadly voice while Jake swore quietly. All he could think about was Maggie driving the pickup, which she did constantly. Maggie and Katy. He wished he could hit Weldon Higgens again.

"Damn," Jake said, glancing at the house. "Maggie will want to know."

"You go tell her," Ben said. "Ty, what's he charged with?"

While Ty read the list of charges, Jake headed toward the house, trying to bank his rage at Weldon Higgens. Jake dreaded telling Maggie. Even though the ordeal was over, he suspected the news would shock and worry her.

He found her braiding Katy's hair and he stood in the doorway, watching mother and daughter. Katy's pink room with stuffed bears and fancy dolls made Jake feel out of place. Looking like a big doll herself, Katy perched on a chair, so her mother could braid her hair.

"What's going on in here?" he asked.

"I'm getting my hair fixed like Mommy's," Katy said, smiling at him and he smiled in return, feeling all his anger vanish. What was it with these two females that with just a look they could make him feel better? Their smiles and big blue eyes seemed to hold sunshine.

"Come see my dolly," Katy said. "She has her hair like mine and Mommy's, too. Mommy braided it this morning." She held up a doll and he entered the room, taking the small doll in his hands.

"Your dolly's very pretty, Katy, but not as pretty as you and your Mommy," he said. Maggie wrinkled her nose at him.

Maggie finished and Katy jumped down. "Can I go out with Grandpa?"

Maggie went to the window and raised it to call to her father. "Can Katy come outside with you?"

She turned back and nodded to Katy. "You stay right with Grandpa."

"Yes, ma'am. Can I take my dolly?"

"Yes, you may," Maggie said and watched Katy scamper out of the room. When she turned to the window, Jake sauntered over to stand beside her. In a few minutes he saw Ben take Katy's hand.

"You must be here for a reason," Maggie said, facing Jake and moving away from the window.

"I am. It doesn't matter now, Maggie, because they have Weldon locked up, but he cut the brake lines in the pickup. Whoever drove the pickup next, when the brake fluid leaked out, would have had the brakes go completely."

As she paled, Jake swore. "Damn him. Don't let it scare you or worry you now. He's history."

"I suppose you're right," she said, anger snapping in her blue eyes. "Thanks for telling me and thank goodness you caught him."

He ran his finger along her collar. "Ben's putting his shotgun up in his closet."

"You got Dad to do that!" she exclaimed in exasperation, placing her hand on her hip. "Jake Reiner! You have no business meddling in my life when you probably won't even be around here a year from now."

"Well, maybe and maybe not," he drawled. "But right now I'm here, so I might do a little meddling, darlin'," he said, reaching for her and sliding his arms around her waist. "How are your ribs today? Plenty sore, I'd imagine."

"That's right."

"But not too sore to go out to dinner with me Saturday night. Ben is going to Patsy's this weekend and he said he would take Katy with him."

"You've already worked this all out, haven't you? And I'm the last to know."

"Well, that's because we needed to work out a few details before I could ask you. Otherwise, you'd have to say no because you'd have to stay home to watch Katy. Go to dinner with me, Maggie."

"How can I refuse?" she said, smiling at him.

He kissed her until she pushed him away. "I know where kisses with you end, and we can't go back to bed now. Now scoot."

"Yes, ma'am. About six o'clock Saturday night. Let's get an early start," he said, eagerness making him smile.

As she nodded, he caressed her throat, feeling her pulse race. "I excite you, Maggie," he said, his voice dropping and his temperature climbing. "But not half as much as you excite me."

She inhaled swiftly, and her eyes darkened as they did in moments of passion. He wanted to pull her back into his arms, but he knew he needed to get to work.

Late that night for the first time, after he had put Rogue through his paces, Jake dismounted, opened the corral gate and rode the horse down the lane toward the county road. He was conscious of the horse, but his mind kept wandering to the ring he had tucked away in a drawer in his bedroom.

He didn't expect Maggie to say yes, but if she did, was he absolutely certain that's what he wanted? How would they live? Going from pillar to post and taking Katy with them? Could he be heartless enough to ask her to ever leave Ben? Jake couldn't imagine staying on the Circle A ranch the rest of his life. Or could he? All he knew with certainty was that he had to ask Maggie to marry him and he wanted her desperately.

Saturday night Jake showered and dressed swiftly in a white Western shirt and crisp jeans, too aware that Maggie was just down the hall and Ben and Katy had gone to town. He had Maggie all to himself now. He was half inclined to chuck his plans for the evening, go down the hall and take her to bed and give her the ring later tonight.

Yet he wanted to take her out. He had made elaborate plans to try to do something she would remember and something that would please her.

He opened his drawer and removed the ring box, raising the dark blue lid and staring at the dazzling diamond set against white satin. He couldn't summon an ounce of eagerness because he was unsure of her reaction. He removed the ring, wrapped it in a bit of tissue and jammed it into his pocket, wondering if he would even give it to her tonight.

Her door stood open and he hurried downstairs to find her in the kitchen, talking on the phone to Katy. Pausing in the doorway, he let his gaze drift over her appreciatively. She was in a red dress and all he wanted to do was go peel her out of it. It was made of some kind of material that clung to her curves. Sleeveless, the dress left her slender arms bare and it was short, leaving a good portion of very shapely legs showing. She wore high-heeled red pumps and she looked sexy and delectable. Watching him, she replaced the receiver.

"Hi, handsome," she drawled seductively as she hung up the phone, making his pulse accelerate another notch. His throat closed up while the world vanished. All he knew was Maggie was too far away from him. He crossed the kitchen to her to wrap his arms around her.

"Lady, I want you," he said, his voice a husky rasp.

Ten

Jake leaned down to kiss her, his arms tightening around her waist. While Maggie's heart thudded, she wrapped her arms around him, feeling his warmth through the crisp cotton shirt that was a dazzling white against his dark-skinned handsomeness.

She opened her mouth to him, taking his scalding kisses that promised so much more. As his fingers dug into her shoulder, he leaned over her, one hand sliding over her bottom and pulling her up against him. He wasn't hiding how badly he wanted her. His desire and his kisses made her tremble and melt into his arms. She wanted him as urgently, kissing him hungrily and taking what he was offering of himself.

He straightened to look down at her. As fire blazed in his eyes, she slid her hands across his broad shoulders, moving to the buttons of his shirt, wanting to get closer to him and have all barriers gone. When he caught her hands, she looked up in surprise.

"We're going to take time tonight, Maggie. I want to savor you and the evening with you. We haven't had too many times out together and we need some more memories."

She ran her fingers across his chest. "I don't mind not going out."

He inhaled, causing his chest to expand while his gaze burned into her. "I'm trying, Maggie, to make this a night for you to remember. Help me out here."

"Whatever you want, Jake," she said, thrilled by his words and excited, knowing they would come home and make love the rest of the night. She turned to head to the door and he caught her wrist, spinning her around into his arms to kiss her hungrily as if he would devour her right here and now. As she wrapped her arms around his neck and clung to him, her pulse raced. When he ground his hips against her, she felt his manhood and knew he wanted her. He raised his head. "This is what I want. You, Maggie, naked in my arms, your softness taking me and shutting out the world."

His voice was a breathless rasp, and he kissed her again before he released her. "If we're going, we better get the hell gone. Another minute of your kisses and we won't leave this house."

She looked at him, debating, knowing he had plans for them, yet wanting to love all night long. "C'mon, cowboy. Show me what you have planned. And bring me home early."

He groaned. "Early wasn't part of it, but we'll do what we can."

While he kept her hand on his knee, he drove to the Stillwater airport.

"There's a restaurant here?" Maggie asked, staring at the planes and runway.

"Nope. I've chartered a plane and a pilot to fly you out of Oklahoma."

"Do Dad and Patsy know where to find me?"

"Of course, they do."

Maggie felt a mixture of reactions, turning to him and smiling. "Where are you taking me?"

"As close as I can get in one evening to an ocean. I've chartered a small jet and a pilot to fly us to Houston where we'll rent a car. We'll eat in Galveston on the Gulf. It'll be black as midnight, but you'll see the Gulf and you will finally have been outside of Oklahoma."

She leaned forward to throw her arms around his neck. "Jake, thank you! For my first trip out of state, I'm glad you're with me. But we won't have much time tonight at home."

"We'll do the best we can with what we have," he said, grinning at her, but she had a scary premonition that they were running out of time together.

Everything was a wonder to her and as the small jet lost altitude, coming in to land, she gazed at the twinkling lights of Houston. Unable to sit still and talking nonstop to Jake, she knew this was old stuff to him. Yet he kept grinning and seemed pleased that she was thrilled by all of it.

"Jake, it's just gorgeous." She turned to kiss him, long and deeply, wrapping one arm around his neck to hold him close. She pulled away. "I'll never forget this night!"

"I hope not, Maggie," he replied solemnly, and her heart turned over.

In a rental car they drove to Galveston, and she was so excited, she was still fidgety and talking constantly. "I'm being silly, I know, but this is exciting."

"I'm glad," he said, sounding pleased. In Galveston they drove along the highway next to the seawall and she could see whitecaps as the waves rolled in. As she listened to breakers splash against the seawall, she inhaled the fresh air. "Oh, Jake! I can't believe we're here!"

"We're here, Maggie." He stopped in the parking lot of a restaurant. Neon light played over him when he turned to face her. "I'll give you a choice. I've made reservations here for us for a candlelight dinner and then I planned a walk on the beach. Or we can get something in Houston to take on the plane. It might not be as fancy, but it'll be hotter than if we get something here and take it back."

"Let's get something in Houston."

"Good enough. C'mon. I have to cancel some reservations."

In minutes he drove them to a stretch of sandy beach. The water was rough and even though it stretched away in inky blackness, she was thrilled. She could see occasional white caps near the shore and they walked hand in hand while she inhaled deeply. "Jake, I love this."

He laughed. "You can't see a damn thing."

"I don't care. I know it's there and I can see a little glimmer."

"We could spend the night here and you could see

it at dawn. That's the best. The tide will be going out and there'll be shells.''

She shook her head. "This is enough for now. I want to go home with you tonight.''

"Come here," he said in a husky voice and pulled her to him to kiss her. He was warm while the cool wind coming off the water tugged at her hair and she held him tightly until he released her.

"Thanks, Jake, for giving me this night.''

"Sure." He took her hand. "Take your shoes off and we'll wade out," he said as he sat in the sand and yanked off his boots. He rolled up his jeans several inches.

"Is it safe to wade at night?''

"It's shallow here and this isn't jellyfish season or they'd be all over the beach. C'mon, just a little ways. I'll keep you safe.''

She knew he would. Kicking off her shoes, she waded out with him. While cold water swirled around her ankles, she thought about where the water would go, exotic places so far away. She listened to the splash as waves came in and loved every moment. Inhaling deeply, she wanted to store up all the memories she could: the smell and feel of the Gulf waters, the grainy sand squishing between her toes, Jake's warm fingers laced through hers, his kisses still warm on her lips.

"Jake, I love this!" she told him again, turning to kiss him while they stood with water swirling around their ankles. "I wish I could bottle some up and take it home and keep it forever.''

He laughed. "It's just sea water, Maggie.''

"It's special because it's the first time I've seen it

and I'm here with you. Those are two reasons to want to keep a bit of memories forever.''

''Ah, lady, what you do to me,'' he said, pulling her to him to kiss her again.

Finally they waded out and returned to the car. Jake drove to the other side of the island so Maggie could see the shrimp boats. Before they left Galveston, Jake phoned ahead and ordered steak dinners and they ate on the plane while she watched the lights of Houston fade behind them.

It was long after midnight when they locked the door behind them at home. The moment Jake turned, she moved close, wrapping her arms around him. ''Tonight has been wonderful, but this is the best part,'' she whispered. ''And I've been waiting since we left here earlier.''

He inhaled and leaned down to kiss her, wrapping his strong arms around her as his mouth opened hers and his tongue played with hers.

''I've waited too long tonight, darlin'.''

Their breathing was ragged when he picked her up and carried her upstairs to her room and kicked the door closed behind him. He set her on her feet to turn her around and slowly tug the zipper of her dress down, trailing kisses over her back.

Cool air spilled over her shoulders while his kisses were warm and tantalizing, stirring fiery tingles in their wake. She turned to tug at his belt, sliding it away and reaching up to unfasten his shirt.

As he pushed her dress away, it fell around her ankles, and he inhaled deeply. His hands cupped her breasts while his thumbs circled her nipples. Maggie moaned with pleasure, her body responding to him.

The evening had been a wonder; now it became even more important.

"Ah, Maggie, you're beautiful," he whispered. He released the catch to her bra and shoved it away, bending to take her nipple in his mouth and stroke the taut bud with his tongue.

Shaking with urgency, she pushed off his shirt and attempted to unbutton his jeans. In minutes they had shed clothes and Jake picked her up to carry her to bed.

He sat down, cradling her in his arms while he kissed her. When he raised his head, she stroked his jaw, feeling the faintest stubble. "I love you, Jake." Whether wise or foolish, for better or for worse, she loved him with all her heart. Without answering her, he kissed her hard, driving thought from her mind while she clung to his lean, powerful body and shook with need. She wanted all of him, wanting to take him into her softness, wanting his strength, wanting for even a few moments to feel that he was hers.

Jake shifted, laying her on the bed and moving over her to trail kisses from her throat to her breast while he caressed her. She moaned, her hands moving over him. As he kissed her, he watched her. Her long hair was fanned out on the pillow with a few strands lying on her shoulders.

"You're beautiful," he repeated, thinking he would never tire of looking at her. She was breathtakingly beautiful. She had just told him she loved him, and he felt awed and humbled that he had won her love. And the last thing he ever wanted to do in any way was hurt her.

And now, some things in the world he was seeing through her eyes. He had been to the Gulf too many times to count in his life, but until tonight, it had never seemed special. It was sea water, wide and open with sandy beaches and a small island town and seaport. But tonight the beach and water had been touched by magic, the magic of Maggie's delight. And now, for the next few hours, she was his and he was intoxicated with her. He wanted to drive her beyond the brink of control. For this night he wanted to make her his, because for the first time in his life, he was truly and deeply in love.

He trailed kisses along her inner thigh and then moved intimately between her legs, until she was thrashing wildly and tugging at him. "Jake, please. I want you!"

He struggled to maintain his control, waiting as long as he could before he slowly lowered himself into her. As she enveloped him, he cried her name while his control vanished.

Maggie held Jake, trailing her arms down his smooth back and over his firm buttocks, feeling the rough hairs on the backs of his muscled thighs. He was solid planes, hard where she was soft, fascinating to her.

"Maggie, my love!" he cried, and her hips rose, meeting his. Clinging to him, she moved with him, but his words were ecstasy to her. *My love!* She relished those two words. He did love her.

Joy heightened every sensation and the moment was etched in her heart and memory. Conscious thoughts spun away as her urgency grew.

"Jake," she cried, moving wildly with him, her pulse drowning out sounds. She cried out, arching her back, bursting with release and feeling him shudder with his own earth-shaking climax.

They both sagged, slowing and trying to regain their breath.

Jake showered light kisses on her forehead and cheek and the corner of her mouth, shifting beside her and turning her into his arms to hold her close. Listening to his heart slow, she stroked his back that was damp with sweat.

"I love you," she said softly, knowing that no matter what tomorrow might bring, she would love him forever.

"Darlin'," he whispered, kissing her lightly. His hands moved over her. "I feel like it's been a thousand years since I held you like this."

She leaned back to look at him, placing her palm on his cheek. "Thanks for tonight. It was special in every way."

"I want to make it more special," he whispered, brushing a kiss on her forehead. He slipped out of bed and picked her up, carrying her to the shower. They showered and made love again and lay in the dim light talking until Jake slid out of bed and walked over to find his jeans.

"I have a surprise," he said as he dug in his pocket.

"Oh?" Maggie sat up against pillows and pulled the sheet high under her arms.

Jake slid beneath the sheet and scooted over to sit by her, his knee against her hip. He looked solemn and she wondered what the surprise was. One fist was clenched and she studied him, unable to discern any hint from his expression.

"Open your hand. I have something I want to give you."

She held out her hand, still mystified, wondering

if he had gotten her a necklace because there were few things small enough to fit in his fist. Yet he seemed far too solemn and now, as he stared at her, she was puzzled. "What is it?" she asked, smiling at him.

"I love you, Maggie." With a surge of joy, she watched as he took her hand in his and opened his fist. A sparkling diamond tumbled into her palm. "Will you marry me?" he asked.

Stunned, she looked up at him. "You want to get married?" she whispered. Her first reaction was pure joy. She took the ring and slipped it onto her finger and threw her arms around his neck. "Oh, Jake!" She kissed him and his arm went around her waist, hauling her into his arms as he kissed her hungrily.

He released her and looked down at her solemnly and her heart thudded because he was too somber. She sat up, tugging the sheet up tightly under her arms while she looked at the ring and then at him. And then reason began to assail her, and she knew why he looked so solemn. Dread started as a tiny icicle of fear and then mushroomed into a coldness that turned her entire heart to ice.

"There are some questions and things to discuss before I can give you an answer," she said.

"I thought there would be," he said. In that moment she knew that he wanted her to marry him, but he didn't want to change his vagabond lifestyle.

"Jake, I have to think of Katy and Dad and the ranch. It's not just me."

"I know that."

She looked at the ring on her finger. Even in the dim light, the diamond sparkled, catching and giving off tiny lights, yet not enough sparkle to chase away the shadows. "If we marry, would you settle here?"

As he drew a deep breath, his gaze met hers and he shook his head. "Maggie, I can't promise that."

"How can you want to marry then?" she cried. "You want Katy and me to ride across the country on your bike? Jake, she'll start kindergarten this year and then she'll be in school." Something inside Maggie shattered, and a dull pain started.

"Maggie, for now I'm happy here, but I can't promise that I won't have to move on to something else someday. I can't promise that I'll take root here like you have. Kids move and change schools and I can stop moving as much, but to promise to stay forever—I just can't do it," he said.

"You know I can't leave my dad now."

"I know and I'm not asking you to now. I'm just being honest enough to tell you that I can't promise to stay here forever."

"Dad's health isn't good, but it isn't terrible, either. He could live for years, and it wouldn't be any easier to leave five years from now than now. Probably harder to leave. Katy would have her friends. If you love us, why can't you stay?"

He moved impatiently and a muscle worked in his jaw. "There just comes a time when I have to keep moving. I get so damned restless and penned in."

"And scared to love," she said softly. "When you really begin to care, I'll bet that's when you move on."

"I don't know about that." He reached out, sliding his hand behind her curtain of hair. "I just know that I love you and I want you in my life." He leaned forward and kissed her long and hard, but all the time she kissed him back, she knew it was impossible. Hot tears stung and she tasted their salt.

"Ah, Maggie, dammit," he whispered, wiping away her tears with his thumbs. "I don't want to hurt you. But you don't want me to give you all kinds of promises I can't keep."

"No, I don't." She wrapped her arm around his neck and kissed him and he pulled her down into his embrace, rolling her onto her back and moving over her.

"I love you so damned much," he whispered and kissed her.

But not enough to stay with me, she thought. She kissed him, wanting him with the same hungry desperation she had felt earlier in the evening, knowing she was losing him even as she loved him.

They made love far into the early hours of morning and then slept in each other's arms. When she stirred, Jake was gone and she showered and dressed to go searching for him. She found him in the kitchen with breakfast cooked.

They ate scrambled eggs and toast and talked, but there was a somber knowledge that hung in the air and had changed their relationship.

After breakfast, she sat facing him across the table. Feeling as if she were tearing her heart out and giving it to him, she slowly pulled the ring off her finger. When she held out the ring, she looked into his eyes. "Here, Jake. I can't take your ring. This is my home, and I have to stay here with my family."

"Maggie, I'd never take you away from them forever. We could come back."

She shook her head. "No. I can't do that to Dad. Would you really want me to leave him?"

Jake stared at her. "I guess that's why I've known all along what your answer would have to be, but I love you so much it hurts. I had to ask you."

She closed her eyes in pain and fought tears, wanting to avoid crying again in front of him.

When she opened her eyes and stood, he came around the table swiftly to reach for her, but she stepped back. "Have you ever thought that if you loved someone, life might be different? You might not feel that urge to keep moving?"

"I don't know. I just don't feel that I can promise I'll change."

"And I can't promise anything, either," she whispered and spun around to leave the room. Knowing their weekend was over, she raced upstairs, tears blurring her path. So much was over. She heard the back door and guessed he had gone outside.

In her room she went to the window and watched his long stride eat up the ground as he headed toward the barn and disappeared inside.

She touched her ring finger where Jake's diamond had rested so briefly. "I love you now and I always will no matter where you are or what you do," she whispered, knowing that if he left, she couldn't stop loving him. Nor could she ever take up Jake's way of living.

Two hours later Maggie left for church. Jake watched her drive away and swore under his breath. He had put the ring away in a small knapsack in the bottom of a drawer in his bedroom. He didn't want to think about the future. Always before, tomorrows had taken care of themselves, and he hadn't given much thought to the rest of his life. Now he didn't want to think about the future without Maggie.

He hurt and he suspected the hurt was just starting and was something he would have to live with for a long time.

He mounted Rogue, knowing that he would have to concentrate on the horse and that it would take his mind from the early hours of the morning and the woman he loved.

It was a week later when Maggie came down for breakfast and found Jake already sipping black coffee and orange juice. A bowl of strawberries was on the table.

"Thanks for cooking breakfast," she said, her pulse accelerating at the sight of him in jeans, a T-shirt and his black boots. He had been avoiding her more and more lately, just as she had tried to stay away from being alone with him. He stood and gazed at her solemnly. One look into his eyes and she knew something was wrong.

"I've been wanting to talk to you," he said quietly.

As Maggie's heart lurched, she was filled with dread.

Eleven

He came across the room and with each step closer, her heartbeat speeded up. Stopping only a foot away, he placed his hands on her shoulders. "I love you, Maggie. I love Katy and Ben and this place, but seeing you every day and wanting you in my arms and my bed, knowing I can't have—that's hell."

"Oh, Jake," she whispered, thinking if he loved all of them, there was a simple solution.

"I've never stayed anywhere long. Never once in my whole life. My folks moved a lot and even when I was a kid, I was a roamer. I'm going because this is bad for both of us."

Closing her eyes, she felt enveloped in pain. She always knew he would go, but she didn't know how badly it would hurt. She opened her eyes, wrapped her arms around his neck and stood on tiptoe, pulling his head down and placing her mouth on his to kiss him with all the pent-up longing she had been suffering this past week.

His arm banded her waist and he crushed her against his chest while he kissed her as if it were the last kiss he would ever have.

She tasted salty tears and didn't care. She loved him desperately and wanted him. She stepped back. "If you love me and you love my family, why can't you stay?"

"This hurts every day, Maggie. I want you as my wife."

"You know why I can't marry you. It doesn't have to be this way." Hurting, she stepped back. "Go on, then. Jake, you're running from the guilt you have over your brothers and parents dying when you didn't die with them, but you didn't have one thing to do with the fire or their deaths."

"I'm not running from that!" he snapped. "And I might have saved them if I'd been there."

"Jake, life is full of 'ifs,' but the truth is that you weren't there. You're running from guilt over something you shouldn't feel guilty about."

"Like hell."

"Go on. Just go," she said, hurting for herself and for both of them. He was a wonderful man and he shouldn't lead a solitary life because of something that wasn't his fault.

"I want to tell Katy and Ben goodbye."

"Then do it without me. I'll say goodbye now." They stared at each other, each caught in an impasse that she knew was unresolvable as long as he felt the way he did. "Can't you see what you're doing to yourself, and it's so needless. Let go of guilt. Let go of the past and live life fully. When you get to the point where you do, you run.''

''Maggie, you're wrong.''

''Goodbye, Jake,'' she said, leaving the room in a rush. She yanked up her jacket and went out to get into the pickup. Ben would take care of Katy and Jake would stay until they both woke up. For once, Maggie was going to give herself some time and space and privacy. She drove away without looking back, hurting and wondering if the pain would ever ease.

When she returned two hours later, Ben met her at the back door and stepped outside, closing the door behind him.

''We told Jake goodbye.''

''Daddy, he asked me to marry him, but he couldn't promise to stay here. I can't leave—it isn't you. I can't have that kind of life for Katy.''

Ben stepped forward and wrapped his arms around her. ''Ah, Maggie, I'm sorry. I guess I shouldn't have ever asked him to work for us.''

''No. I'm glad he did. I love him, but I couldn't live the way he does.'' She held her father, glad for his comfort, knowing she was right, yet hurting in a way she had never hurt before.

She moved away. ''I'm all right. What about Katy?''

''She's in there crying her eyes out because she loves him. He's become a father to her, but children adapt. By afternoon she'll be all right. I told her I'd take her to town to see the latest Disney release.''

''Thanks,'' Maggie said, smiling at him. ''I don't know what I'd do without you.''

''And I don't know what I'd do without you. I'm

sorry, honey. I wouldn't want you to stay just for me, but I can see where Katy fits into the equation and gives you reason to say no. Maggie, maybe he'll come back."

She shook her head. "No, he won't. He's been this way all his life and he's thirty-five years old. He isn't going to change now. I'll recover."

Ben draped his arm across her shoulders. "I'm sure you will. I wonder if Jake will."

When they went inside, Maggie had to reassure Katy and comfort her when all she wanted to do was cry right along with her daughter. She hurt and she missed Jake.

That night she didn't sleep, crying until there were no tears left, wondering if he was hurting, too, or just going on with his life as he had done times before.

Jake sat in a dark motel room in Kansas. He had crossed the state line and he didn't know or care where he was. For the first time since he was fourteen, he bought a six-pack of beer. He slammed down two bottles and threw the rest in the trash. Sitting at the window, he stared at the empty swimming pool and hurt more than he had ever hurt in his life. He stared at still blue water, but all he could see were blue eyes filled with love.

Was she right? Was he running away from guilt that he shouldn't be suffering?

How hard would it be to let go of the past? Was he running again as he had that night—running away from his family and consequently losing all of them. Now he was running again and he was losing a family that could be his if he would just let them.

"Maggie," he whispered hoarsely into the darkness. "I love you. I want you."

He swore and stood up, pacing the dark room and then he stuffed his billfold into his pocket and looked at himself in the mirror. "Who are you?" he asked his reflection, wondering who he was and what he was doing.

He picked up his keys and went out, locking the motel room behind him. He had already paid his bill. Climbing onto his bike, he revved the engine, shattering the stillness of the crisp fall night. He didn't care. He turned the bike and drove out of the motel lot, heading for the highway and turning south.

It was four in the morning when Maggie heard the roar of the Harley. Her heart thudded and excitement shook her as she ran for the door and raced down the stairs and went outside.

When Jake drove up to the back gate, she thought she would faint from joy. Was he a dream? She ran toward him as he vaulted the fence and ran to grab her up in his strong arms, swinging her around and kissing her hard enough that she knew he was no dream. He was flesh and blood, and her heart thudded.

While he still held her off the ground, she raised her head and framed his face with her hands. "Why are you here?"

"You might have been right. To hell with the past. I can't live without you, Maggie."

"Oh, Jake," she said, melting. Joy bubbled in her as she kissed him and clung to him tightly.

"You're my special woman, darlin'," he said. "Marry me, Maggie. I'll stay. I'll take root here like you and Ben and these damn trees. In a few years you won't be able to get me ten miles from here. Will you marry me?''

''Yes! Oh, yes! I love you!'' she answered while she laughed and cried at the same time. ''Jake, I love you,'' she said and kissed him, barely aware that he had swung her up into his arms and was carrying her toward the barn.

''Come on, darlin'. We have some lovin' to catch up on,'' he whispered as he showered kisses over her face.

Epilogue

As his boot heels scraped the bare floor, Jake moved close to the hospital bed. Over an hour earlier, on the second day of April, a year after their fall wedding, he had helped as Maggie gave birth to a seven pound boy. Now Katy was with them and Maggie held the sleeping infant, wrapped in a blue blanket, in the crook of her arm.

Sitting down beside Maggie, Jake lifted Katy onto his lap. With a sparkle in her eyes and her hair spilling over her shoulders and blue gown, Maggie had never looked more beautiful to him. As his arm tightened around Katy, he looked at his new son, his little daughter and his radiant wife. A knot thickened Jake's throat while tears filled his eyes. "Darlin', you've given me a family."

"Jake," Maggie said softly, reaching for him, sliding her arm around his neck and pulling him closer, hugging Katy and careful of the baby at the same time.

He kept one arm around Katy and the new baby, Matthew, while he held Maggie with his other arm. "Darlin', I love all three of you. I can't tell you how much."

"I love you," she whispered, stroking his head, and he realized how blessed he was with this wonderful family that he had been given.

"Knock, knock," came a deep voice, and Jake straightened, trying to get control of his emotions and wiping his eyes as he turned to look into the gaze of his friend, Jeb Stuart.

"I'll come back later," Jeb said, backing up and closing the door behind him.

"Hey!" Jake jumped up and Katy followed him into the hall where he saw Jeb and the rest of the Stuarts.

"Come in," Jake said, shaking hands with Jeb and turning to hug Amanda.

"How's Maggie and the new baby?" Jeb asked as Jake hugged each of the Stuart children.

"They're both doing great. Come see him."

When Jake knocked lightly on the door before putting his head inside, Maggie smiled. "Tell everyone to come in," she said, looking at her handsome husband as Jake led the way. He wore his hair shorter now, but he still had that streak of wildness that showed in his rugged features and his lively dark eyes. All five Stuarts followed him into the room and Maggie greeted them and showed them the new baby.

"We've named him Matt for Jake's youngest brother," Maggie said, smiling at Jake.

"He's beautiful," Amanda exclaimed.

"Boys aren't beautiful," Jeb teased and she gave him a haughty look.

"Baby boys are," she said, leaning over the bed.

"You may hold him if you want," Maggie said.

Amanda carefully took the sleeping baby into her arms. She stepped back and said, "We brought Matthew a present."

Both boys set a large box beside the bed.

"Katy, why don't you unwrap it," Jake said. Grinning, Katy began to peel away ribbon and paper until she finally stepped back to look at a large box.

"It's a swing!" Katy exclaimed in delight, her small fingers sliding over the picture on the box. "Can we open it?"

Thanking the Stuarts, Jake laughed and took the box from her. "It might be better to open it at home where I can set it up for Matt."

"Katy, here's something for you," Amanda said and Emily held out another present, which Katy unwrapped swiftly, tossing aside colorful paper.

"A book!" She held up a book and ran her fingers over the title, reading it aloud.

"What do you say, Katy?" Maggie prompted.

"Thank you," she said, grinning at the Stuarts. "Let's read it," she told Emily and the two girls hurried across the room to a sofa to sit with their heads together, Katy slowly reading to Emily.

By ten o'clock that night, Patsy had taken Katy home with her and Ben had gone back to Patsy's. The Stuarts had left and all the other visitors were gone. Jake was sleeping on the sofa in Maggie's room and he sat on the bed beside her, holding her hand and smiling at her.

"Oh, Jake! It's so wonderful!" She held out her arms and he leaned forward to gather her gently into his embrace. Maggie held him, feeling his heart beat against hers. When she looked at the sleeping infant in the nearby crib, joy brought tears to her eyes. "I'm the luckiest person in the world."

"Sorry, darlin', that person is me," Jake said gruffly, holding her close. Maggie closed her eyes, knowing Jake's roaming was over and he would stay in her arms for the rest of their lives.

* * * * *

Silhouette *Desire*®

presents

DYNASTIES: THE CONNELLYS

A brand-new miniseries about the Connellys of Chicago,
a wealthy, powerful American family tied by blood to the
royal family of the island kingdom of Altaria.
They're wealthy, powerful and rocked by
scandal, betrayal...and passion!

Look for a whole year of glamorous and
utterly romantic tales in 2002:

Silhouette®

Where love comes alive™

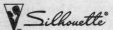

Three bold, irresistible men.
Three brand-new romances by today's top authors...
Summer never seemed hotter!

Sheiks of Summer

*Available in August
at your favorite
retail outlet!*

"The Sheik's Virgin" by Susan Mallery

He was the brazen stranger who chaperoned innocent, beautiful
Phoebe Carson around his native land. But what would Phoebe do when
she discovered her suitor was none other than Prince Nasri Mazin—
and he had seduction on his mind?

"Sheikh of Ice" by Alexandra Sellers

She came in search of adventure—and discovered passion in the arms
of tall, dark and handsome Hadi al Hajar. But once Kate Drummond
succumbed to Hadi's powerful touch, would she succeed in
taming his hard heart?

"Kismet" by Fiona Brand

A star-crossed love affair and a stormy night combined to bring
Laine Abernathy into Sheik Xavier Kalil Al Jahir's world. Now, as she
took cover in her rugged rescuer's home, Lily wondered if it was her
destiny to fall in love with the mesmerizing sheik....

**Where royalty and romance
go hand in hand...**

The series continues in Silhouette Romance
with these unforgettable novels:

HER ROYAL HUSBAND
by Cara Colter
on sale July 2002 (SR #1600)

THE PRINCESS HAS AMNESIA!
by Patricia Thayer
on sale August 2002 (SR #1606)

SEARCHING FOR HER PRINCE
by Karen Rose Smith
on sale September 2002 (SR #1612)

And look for more Crown and Glory stories in
SILHOUETTE DESIRE starting in October 2002!

Available at your favorite retail outlet.

Where love comes alive™

COMING NEXT MONTH

SDCNM0702